NORBY AND THE OLDEST DRAGON

"Ma'am, we've come to visit you because—"

"It's outrageous!" the oldest dragon said, puffing another cloud of smoke at Jeff that made him cough. "I thought that going to the farthest and coldest island of Jamya would ensure my privacy but after only fifty years of retirement I'm intruded upon like this. . . . Go away, alien monster, and take that sawed-off version of a robot with you."

"I am a perfect size and shape!" Norby yelled back.

ABOUT THE AUTHORS

JANET ASIMOV is the author of *Mind Transfer*, *The Second Experiment*, and *The Last Immortal* as well as many short stories and articles.

ISAAC ASIMOV wrote more than four hundred books including the bestselling *The Robots of Dawn* and *Foundation*. He created the famous "Laws of Robotics." Janet and Isaac Asimov were married in 1973, and collaborated on all of the acclaimed "Norby" novels.

Isaac Asimov died in 1992.

PRAISE FOR THE "NORBY" ADVENTURES

"A charming set of characters . . . unique adventures."   —*School Library Journal*

"As usual, the Asimovs have crowded history, science, and a good yarn into a few short pages."

—*Kirkus Reviews*

"Robotic fans and those who enjoyed Norby's earlier adventures will find this fast-paced plot equally diverting . . . funny!"   —*Booklist*

Ace Books by Janet and Isaac Asimov

THE NORBY CHRONICLES
NORBY: ROBOT FOR HIRE
NORBY THROUGH TIME AND SPACE
NORBY AND YOBO'S GREAT ADVENTURE
NORBY DOWN TO EARTH
NORBY AND THE OLDEST DRAGON

NORBY AND THE OLDEST DRAGON

JANET AND ISAAC ASIMOV

ACE BOOKS, NEW YORK

All characters and events portrayed
in this story are fictitious.

This Ace book contains the complete text of the original
hardcover edition. It has been completely reset in a typeface
designed for easy reading, and was printed from new film.

NORBY AND THE OLDEST DRAGON

An Ace Book / published by arrangement with
Walker and Company

PRINTING HISTORY
Walker and Company edition published 1990
Published simultaneously in Canada by Thomas Allen & Son
Ace edition / January 1993

ISBN: 0-441-58632-5

Ace Books are published by The Berkley Publishing Group,
200 Madison Avenue, New York, New York 10016.
The name "ACE" and the "A" logo
are trademarks belonging to Charter Communications, Inc.

PRINTED IN THE UNITED STATES OF AMERICA

10 9 8 7 6 5 4 3 2 1

This book is in honor of two delightful
new relatives, born in the spring of 1989—

Sarah Elizabeth Jeppson
Emily Bennetts Gerard

1

Dress Uniforms

Cadet Jefferson Wells was having a difficult time packing his suitcase because his room at Space Academy was crowded with three other cadets bubbling with curiosity and questions about Jeff's secret destination.

Norby was no help, either. Although he didn't ask questions because he knew where they were going, he was trying to impress the other cadets with the fact that he was an efficient personal robot in spite of being small, barrel-shaped, and having only half a head. Waving his extensible arms, Norby gave advice. Lots of advice.

"Jeff, don't put your spare boots on the bottom because everything on top will get lumpy. Put them into the spaces left when you've finished everything else. And don't forget to pack your new toothpastebrush because the one in the suitcase is empty. And I recommend at least two extra pairs of socks because the last time we went anywhere you didn't even have one to change into . . ."

As Norby droned on and the other cadets laughed, Jeff rebelliously put in only one extra pair of socks. After all, they were only going for the weekend.

Although he was an orphaned fifteen-year-old, Jeff had managed to survive many dubious adventures, most of them caused by the fact that his so-called teaching robot contained weird alien parts and mixed everything up at unexpected moments. He resolved that the trip for which he was now packing would be purely for pleasure, with no duties, no distress, no danger, and no damp socks.

"Jeff, you're not listening," Norby said, louder.

"I'm trying to decide if this dress uniform looks okay on me. I think I've grown some."

"Isn't it about time you stopped growing?" Norby said. "You're bigger than Her Highness as it is . . ."

"Perhaps she'll think you're part orangutan," said the freckled cadet, "what with your wrists dangling like that."

"Don't mind him, Jeff. You still look great in your uniform." That was the female cadet, the one with the smooth brown skin.

"Who is 'Her Highness'?" asked the youngest cadet, whose chubby cheeks grew pinker with curiosity.

" 'Highness' is just a term of . . . of affection," said Jeff, who hated to lie. He shoved a hand through his curly brown hair and scowled at Norby, who wasn't supposed to leak secret information. "We're going to the birthday party of

2

an especially grand old lady."

Norby chuckled metallically, and Jeff had to smile, for although the Grand Dragon of Jamya was definitely grand, she was not particularly old. In fact, considering the way her nostrils literally smoked when Jeff's handsome older brother was around, she was undoubtedly in the prime of life.

The freckled cadet wrinkled his nose. "What a boring thing to have to do. Spend the weekend with us. We're going to play my new version of our favorite computer game, 'Heads Will Roll.' I call it 'Blast Space Command'—"

The girl pummeled him and the youngest joined in, all three falling off the bed onto Jeff's almost packed suitcase.

"Norby! They're ruining my packing!"

Using his powerful, two-way hands, Norby grabbed each of the boys, rose into the air with his mini-antigrav (Federation scientists were still working on duplicating it), and sailed out of the room to deposit them into the hall outside. Before he could return to get the girl, she quickly kissed Jeff and swaggered out, thumbing her nose at Norby on the way.

Jeff finished packing and was sitting on his suitcase so the ownerlock would consent to close, when Norby said, "I bet you forgot to get a present for the Grand Dragon."

"Oh, migosh, I did forget! Maybe I just don't feel like a genuine invited guest to the Grand Dragon's party."

"That's silly, Jeff."

"It isn't. When you returned from Jamya last week you weren't carrying a special, hand-written invitation for me. Only for, and I quote, 'The Marvelous Human, Farley Gordon Wells.' I'm completely aware of the fact that the Grand Dragon told Fargo to bring me along, but only because you're my robot and nobody can go through hyperspace to Jamya without you."

"She told Fargo to bring Albany Jones, too."

"Fargo and Albany are engaged."

"And you're Fargo's kid brother. Are you complaining about it, Jeff?"

"No, of course not." Jeff paused. "Well, maybe. I've always been second, and it's tough being a ten-year-younger second. Albany and Fargo and the Jamyn dragons think I'm still a kid."

"If you were grown up you'd have remembered to buy the Grand Dragon a present."

"Norby!" But he was right. Feeling like a kid indeed, Jeff groaned and said, "Is it too late to buy a present?"

"Don't fret. As a superefficient robot, I have wrapped a present for Her Dragonness and it's in the suitcase's outside compartment. I had a duplicate made of Fargo's picture."

"Thanks, Norby."

"Sorry I didn't get one of you, too, but you haven't liked any of the pictures you've had taken recently and we've always agreed that that one of Fargo is special."

Admiral Yobo's most secret secret agent smiled at them from a holoportrait on the wall, his blue eyes shining and his wavy black hair impeccable. There was no doubt about it, Fargo had the sort of face that made you think of a dashing cavalier whose flair for danger was mitigated by his sense of humor. Jeff couldn't help smiling back at the portrait of his only sibling.

A musical tenor voice interrupted. "I'm glad to see that my little brother appreciates me."

The same handsome, blue-eyed face was grinning from the computer monitor. "I will be even gladder if you would hurry up. Albany and I are at exit dock twelve, with the *Hopeful* champing at the bit, eager to be up, up, and away—if you don't mind a few mixed metaphors."

"Isn't Admiral Yobo with you?" Jeff asked. With the addition of the head of Space Command, all the humans who'd ever been to the distant planet of Jamya would be together.

"He has to spend the weekend arguing with the Federation Council. It seems the Council's putting through awesome alterations in protocol and retirement regulations—to which you've undoubtedly paid no attention due to your extreme youth and inability to imagine it happening to you—and Yobo's very upset, not that he's near retirement but the proposed change in uniform for various degrees of seniority has caught him in a sensitive spot, his bank balance. He just laid out a goodly sum for new dress uniforms—by the way, I trust you are wearing your best one, Jeff."

"This blue one that I'm wearing is my best dress uniform. The trouble is in the arms—they're a little short—I mean the sleeves are."

"Your uniform and arms will have to do. Besides, the dragons think all our clothes are ridiculous. Nevertheless, I think it will pay to wear your fanciest, which I assume is the best.

Her Dragonship has an uncanny ability to discern whether or not we are dressed appropriately for paying court to her exalted station. Now hurry, young one. Tell Norby to pick you up and zip you along."

The screen went blank and before Jeff could object, Norby did pick up him and the suitcase and antigrav'd out into the hall. Dodging cadets, they zoomed through the corridors of the Academy into the great rotating wheel of Space Command, in orbit around Mars.

"Norby, slow down or the patrols will pick us up for speeding."

"I'm in a hurry to get back to Jamya. I want to see my father."

Actually, Norby had two "fathers." One had been the human spacer Moses MacGillicuddy, who found his alien parts in a wrecked spaceship and made a new robot from them. His other father was the Jamyn robot called Mentor First, put in charge of the planet Jamya by the mysterious space travelers called the Others.

"You can hyperjump to Jamya any time to see him. Aren't you going to have to pay court to the Grand Dragon too?"

"Sure, but Mentor First is building a new holovision station for the dragons and I'm going to help him with the finishing touches. You've always underestimated my talent for improving inanimate, brainless devices. The Jamyn robots are good at constructing other robots and repairing computers, but they can't plug into them the way I can, to adjust the innards in a delicate way. I am a very brainy device."

"I suppose you can't get into trouble helping Mentor First with the holov station."

"I never get into trouble."

"Norby!"

"Almost never."

They could see exit dock twelve ahead and, waving from it, Fargo and his fiancée, blond and beautiful Albany Jones.

"Norby, please don't do anything to annoy the Grand Dragon on her birthday. She's got such a temper, you'd better take special care to behave yourself."

"I always do, Jeff."

2

The Glorious Birthday

"A perfect landing, if I do say so myself."

"You're wonderful, Norby." Albany patted the knob on top of Norby's permanently fixed, broad-rimmed hat. This brought a growl from Oola, Fargo's all-purpose pet, who didn't want Albany to stop stroking her green fur.

"Right on target," Fargo said absently as if, in spite of previous experience with Norby's navigation, he expected no less. He was pre-occupied with rewriting the lyrics of the song he'd composed in honor of the birthday.

"Amazing," Jeff said. "There was no trouble getting the *Hopeful* out of Space Command's dock. You channeled your hyperdrive into the ship's computer faultlessly. We entered hyperspace easily. We arrived at Jamya at once, in the right place. I can't understand it—absolutely nothing went wrong."

"You have no faith in me, Jeff," Norby said in

the tinny voice he used when his emotive circuits had been wounded. He detached himself from the controls of the little scout ship and added, "Here comes the welcoming committee."

In the viewscreen, Mentor First's black metal body shone as if it had just been polished, and in the distance behind him the light of Jamya's sun also reflected from the large castle of the robots. Mentor First's three eyes glowed with happiness and his lower pair of arms was held out in greeting. The top pair of arms carried an older version of Oola as well as the young dragon Zargl, decked out with a multicolored ribbon looped along the spikes of her tail.

Lugging suitcases, the three humans left the ship followed by Norby carrying Oola, who promptly wriggled out of his grasp and galloped to Mentor First and her mother. Zargl spread her wings and flew over to Fargo with the aid of the gold antigrav collar that all the Jamyn dragons wore.

"Where's Admiral Yobo?" Zargl asked in Terran Basic, which she'd been practicing.

Albany explained in Jamyn, which she needed to practice because she hadn't had much chance to use it since she learned it telepathically—something easy to do once you are gently bitten (for the purpose) by a Jamyn dragon.

"Oh, well," Zargl said, "At least you're here, Fargo. The Grand Dragon has been asking for you. And it's so good that Albany and Jeff could come, too."

They all walked briskly through the trees to the Grand Dragon's palace, which Fargo alone had visited before. Jeff lagged behind, still feeling that he was wanted only because he owned Norby. Until the Federation built a reliable hyperdrive ship, only Norby's hyperdrive could get any human away from the Terran solar system across the galaxy to Jamya. He wished he'd stayed back with the other cadets.

—Don't feel bad, Jeff. [That was Norby, touching his hand and making telepathic contact.]

—Maybe I can help you and Mentor First with the holov equipment instead of having to go to this old birthday party.

—But you're not exactly terrific at electronics, Jeff.

That was true. Jeff was passably good at a great many things but unlike Norby, Fargo, and Albany, he wasn't brilliant at anything. Fargo had once called him "Jack of all trades and master of none," and at the time Jeff was pleased, content to be useful in many small ways. Right now he felt discontented, annoyed with himself and everyone else.

—Well, Norby, I suppose you geniuses won't mind if I watch you work.

—I don't think you should, Jeff. It's not a good idea to insult the Grand Dragon on her special day. I strongly advise you to go to the party.

—Everyone gives me advice but they do exactly what they want and I never can, because as far as everyone is concerned, I'm not yet a grown-up. I'm still in school and don't know exactly what I'm going to do in life, so I suppose I don't have a genuine identity except when I'm with the rest of the cadets.

—But, Jeff . . .

11

—Fargo's got a job, is very musical and a whiz with any female. He enjoys being himself. Albany's one of the best Manhattan cops, besides being beautiful and awfully nice. Even Oola, although she shape-changes to please the person she's with, is still just an animal who enjoys life. And ever since the Mentor robots bioengineered the ancestors of the dragons to reproduce by budding, they've stayed the same and they like that.

—What you're saying, Jeff, is that everyone seems content with the way they are, except you. But you'll grow out of it. Just try to enjoy yourself.

—Oh, leave me alone!

Conscious that he'd never quite said those words to Norby before, Jeff shook off Norby's hand so the little robot wouldn't catch any of his thoughts. Feeling unhappy and very guilty, he plodded up the marble steps to the broad terrace in front of the palace.

On the terrace were many statues of former Grand Dragons, looking insufferably pleased with themselves. Jeff glared at them and believed that all he wanted was to be an ordinary boy, doing the ordinary things other cadets did.

But I've never had an ordinary life, he thought. Not since Mom and Dad died in the ship explosion and Fargo had to bring me up. When I bought Norby in that secondhand robot store, things got a lot better, and we've had great times, but then I see the contented dragon mothers and daughters living their peaceful Jamyn lives . . .

Jeff's thoughts came to an abrupt halt, because it had just occurred to him that perhaps he was finding Jamya too placid. Almost boring.

The Grand Dragon's palace was on top of a slight hill, looking down on the miniature castles where the rest of the dragons lived, scattered over the countryside. The palace did, however, look up to the huge castle of the Mentors, on a much higher hill. From the terrace Jeff could see the purplish ocean of Jamya in the distance, and on the land— a continent smaller than Australia—were fields and woods and many lakes.

Even Jamya's weather was predictable and pleasant, raining softly about twice a week, late at night. Nothing exciting.

"Come on, Jeff!" Fargo shouted from the palace doorway. "Stop mooning about on the front terrace. All the festivities are in the back and we're having a tour of the palace on the way. I want Albany to see everything."

Norby ascended to Mentor First's broad upper shoulder and peered down at Jeff, his emotive circuits obviously agitated for he blinked rapidly a few times. "Father and I are going back to the Mentors' castle now, Jeff. I hope you have a good time at the party."

"Well, I'll *try*." As he said it, Jeff realized it sounded petulant, as if he were planning not to try.

"Enjoy yourselves," Mentor First said in his deep voice. "Norby and I will come later to report on our progress."

"Don't eat too much, Jeff," Norby said.

Jeff shrugged and didn't answer, feeling worse than ever.

The baggage of the human guests was taken from them, and Zargl's mother, Zi, arrived. She conducted them through the palace with such enthusiastic thoroughness that by the time the tour was almost over, Jeff was exhausted with trying to look interested and cheerful. He noticed that Albany and Fargo tactfully did not mention that the various ancient royal families in the Federation had once owned bigger palaces.

In a long gallery full of paintings, Zi pointed to the last and largest of the pictures. "This is my grandmother. The present Grand Dragon was her first bud, and my mother the second. She was perhaps the most delicately beautiful of all the Grand Dragons—small, slender, and such a pale green. I remember her well."

"She was beautiful. When did she die?" Albany asked.

"Oh, she's not dead. At least, we assume she isn't. Every dragon's antigrav collar has within it a life monitor that lets the Mentor robots know if the dragon falls sick. They'd have told us if the Dowager Dragon had died."

"But you haven't seen or heard from her?" Fargo asked.

"Not since she retired, fifty years ago, while still in her prime. Well, almost in her prime. Some of the old ones spend their remaining days with family, continuing their various careers in art or music, but a few choose to become ruolon . . . Zargl—I don't know the Terran word . . ."

"Hermit," Zargl said. "Some silly old ones go off to lonely islands on the other side of the planet. I'd never do a thing like that and miss all the fun here."

"You are a child, dear," Zi said. "We Jamyns

greatly respect those of the old ones who wish to spend their remaining years living simply and practicing meditation. The Dowager is one of the ruolon, in fact the most dedicated of them all. I do hope she is well and happy and will be able to come to this birthday party. She's turned down invitations to all the parties my aunt has had since she became Grand Dragon."

As Zi opened the glass doors at the end of the gallery, Zargl said, "Mother's not telling you just how anxious she and the Grand Dragon are about the Dowager. According to history, none of the previous Grand Dragons became ruolon, but stayed here, enjoying the ceremonies given to Dowager Dragons. It's also most unusual that any ruolon should never leave her island and visit us."

"Now dear," Zi said, moving aside so that the humans could step out onto the back terrace of the palace, "my grandmother was an unusual Grand Dragon in her day, always fragile and too interested in the lonely secrets of the mind. Her meditation is no doubt profound, but I do hope she's remembering to eat and take care of herself."

Albany and Fargo walked out onto the terrace but Jeff stayed behind.

"Didn't the Dowager enjoy being useful when she was the Grand Dragon?" he asked.

"I don't think so. Don't tell my aunt I said this about her mother, but the Dowager always seemed to act as if the rest of us dragons were not good enough, not intelligent or artistic or philosophical enough. She could have stayed on as Grand Dragon for a few more years but chose retirement—and has, as Zargl mentioned, never been back."

Jeff followed her out to the terrace and in spite of his gloomy frame of mind was impressed by the view, for the terrace ended at another broad flight of marble steps leading to a huge arena carpeted by grass and surrounded by gardens. In the exact center of the arena was a fountain with multicolored water jets and multicolored fish in the pool. Lanterns hung in the trees behind the gardens, and low tables had been placed at close intervals over the grass.

"Look at the dragons!" Albany said. "There must be hundreds of them!" They were soaring over the trees, landing gently beside the tables. Each carried a lantern she put by her place at the table, until the entire arena sparkled with light as the sun of Jamya set behind the hills.

"Most of the population comes to the birthday," Zi said.

"That's some party." Fargo cleared his throat. "Do they expect my voice to carry over that oversized football field?"

"Do not worry, dear Fargo," Zargl said, "there is adequate amplification. Our Mentors are up-to-date."

Zi nodded. "We expect that the new holov station will be finished soon. Now that Norby is here, perhaps it will even be working before the festivities begin. Those few dragons who can't make it across our continent to the palace will be able to see and hear the Grand Dragon's speech just as if they were actually here."

Zargl giggled. "The Grand Dragon thinks the

new holov will make government Council meetings take place holographically, but I think everyone will still assemble here for the birthday party, to eat the food. Grandaunt won't save any money."

"I disagree," Zi said. "Too many Jamyn are such homebodies that they hate to travel at all. I think that this may be the last assemblage of the majority of our population. That's why I so hope the Dowager Dragon consents to come. When the message arrives, Mentor First will leave at once in his ship to pick her up."

"How do you communicate with the hermits?" asked Fargo.

"Well," Zi said, "it's not easy because most hermits don't want any technology around them, except their antigrav collars of course. They grow their own gardens and, I believe, gather seaweed and small edible organisms from the ocean. Once a month the Mentors send out an automated rocket that goes to each island and drops messages."

"But the silly old ones won't use the rockets to send messages back," Zargl said. "They use the firebees instead."

"Firebees?" asked Albany. "Something that lives in fire?"

Zargl pointed to a night-blooming flower that was just beginning to open now that dusk was darkening the sky. On the flower was an insect about the size of a Terran bumblebee, but with purple body and wings. From a bulge on the back came an occasional flash of violet light.

"Like fireflies!" Albany exclaimed. "And bees, too!"

"That's why I translated the word that way," Zargl said. "I'm the only Jamyn who's seen your Terran fireflies, but I'm afraid I think our firebees are more beautiful."

"They are," Albany said. "But if they send messages from the hermits by flashing light . . ."

"From island to island and then to the mainland," Zi said, "or if a reply is wanted immediately, they flash to the mail rocket, which relays it back to the Mentors."

"Our Terran fireflies aren't intelligent enough to do that kind of job," Fargo said. "These firebees don't look all that smart either."

"They aren't, individually," Zi said. "But they form a rudimentary hive mind that can receive and send messages. They are the only other species on Jamya, besides us dragons, that has any intelligence to speak of."

"You're not mentioning the sea dragons," Zargl said.

"They're not intelligent. They're horrible, ferocious creatures descended from ancient primitive dragons that adapted to life in the ocean. I do hope the Dowager hasn't been eaten by one of them. She was always fond of swimming. Our lakes are safe, but the ocean is not."

This was the first that Jeff had heard of anything at all dangerous on Jamya. He was intrigued and was about to suggest a trip to the ocean when four dragons rushed out of the palace and positioned themselves at the four corners of the back terrace. They raised oddly shaped trumpets to their mouths and blew a resounding blast of music that silenced everyone.

The dragons at the tables below rose and faced the palace. The humans, Zi, and Zargl backed to one side of the terrace and watched the back door.

The double glass doors opened, the Grand Dragon marched out, and everyone cheered. She looked resplendant in a jeweled gold cape, gem-caps on each of her fangs as well as the spikes on her tail, and rings on almost every claw.

"Her Dragonship has, I'm afraid, gained weight," Fargo whispered. "Just as well if the parties are all by holov from now on. I'm glad she still has a claw left vacant for my birthday present."

He pulled a small box out of the pocket of his fanciest tunic and walked up to the Grand Dragon, while the throng of dragons below drew in their breath sharply. It was unheard of to address royalty before she had given her welcoming speech.

Fargo bowed low and handed the box to the Grand Dragon. She opened it, breathed out a small flame of surprise and joy, and clasped Fargo to her. She was a little taller than he was, so her hot breath singed the top of his hair. He winced but managed to smile beatifically, extricated himself, bowed again, and backed away to Albany and Jeff.

"I gave her a fire opal ring," he muttered in Terran Basic. "They're not terribly expensive on Earth but don't exist here. Flashy enough for Her Dragonship."

The Grand Dragon lifted her wings and her voice boomed out. "Greetings, Jamyn colleagues and beloved human visitors, I am so happy you are here. Have a lovely time at my birthday party." She bowed her head and everyone cheered again.

"That's it? The welcoming speech?" Fargo asked.

"Auntie prefers to look grand and sound humble on her birthday. There will be more speeches later, after we eat, and then you'll sing your song."

The Grand Dragon, her jeweled fangs flashing spectacularly because she was grinning from one scaly ear to the other, waved majestically to the trumpeters. They raised their instruments and another flourish of sound burst forth.

"We shall eat!" the Grand Dragon pronounced, very much like a judge giving a sentence.

"Was that 'we' meaning 'all of us' or 'we' meaning the royal one?" Fargo muttered. "I'm hungry."

"Let's follow auntie," Zi said. "I will walk slightly ahead of you humans because it would not do to have aliens follow closely upon the Grand Dragon."

"Or step on that magnificent cloak," Fargo said. "Besides, Albany and I are familiar with political protocol." Albany's mouth twitched because the mayor of Manhattan, who happened to be her father, was anything but royal.

As Zi led the little group down the marble stairs after the Grand Dragon, Jeff felt that every dragon eye in the throng below was scrutinizing each human. All the Jamyn dragons had heard of the Terrans by now, but many had never seen them.

Zi pointed to the central fountain. "Auntie installed that in place of the swimming pool because she said that after an exceedingly wet adventure with Jeff and Norby[1] she'd had enough of water once the ritual morning shower is completed. The Dowager, when she was Grand Dragon, used the pool for the frequent council meetings we had to have then because the Mentor robots were still paralyzed, rusting in their castle. It was after the Dowager retired that you humans saved the Mentors."[2]

"Excuse me, Zi," Albany said, "but did the former Grand Dragon hold all council meetings beside the swimming pool?"

"Not beside it. *In* it. My grandmother believed that swimming together made it easier to work together."

Fargo raised his black eyebrows. "But what if the water was accidentally swallowed? Wouldn't that put out the firemaking apparatus, or whatever you dragons use biochemically?"

Zi smiled. "I've always believed that was grandmother's purpose. The custom of holding meetings in the swimming pool insured that even the most angry governmental arguments would never get too heated."

"I must tell my father about this," Albany said. "Perhaps an Olympic-sized pool replacing the conference table in City Hall would improve matters, especially since father can outswim anyone on the council."

"Manhattan politics are considerably more dangerous and amusing than anything that happens on Jamya," Fargo said, kissing Albany's rosy cheek.

[1]See "Norby and the Invaders."
[2]**See "Norby's Other Secret."

"Don't forget that once Jamya was a dangerous place," Zi said. "Before the Others left the Mentor Robots here to bioengineer our ancestors, we dragons were a fiercesome bunch of huge predators, the only ones on land because we'd eaten all the others."

"You still have predators in your ocean," Albany said.

Zi looked sad. "Indeed we do, and some of us Jamyn still like to fish, insisting that it's preferable to the synthesized protein and the vat-grown vegetables we eat nowadays. But fishing is a very dangerous pastime. I do worry about the Dowager Dragon. She loved to fish."

They all walked on, arriving at a huge table labeled "Reserved for the Grand Dragon and Guests."

"Auntie is busy saying hello at the other tables, but let's sit down and wait for her." The Terrans sat on the cushions provided for tailless humans incapable of being comfortable in a Jamyn chair.

"I like it here on Jamya," Albany said, gazing around at the scene of happy, convivial dragons. "We Terrans have a much longer history of violence than you dragons, and as a cop I know that the history hasn't ended. You Jamyn are so peaceful, so content with your lives."

Jeff squirmed.

3

The Rejected Invitation

"Have some tsagli." Zargl handed Jeff a purple ball.

"What is it?"

"Special birthday appetizer. Stuffed leaves from a tree that grows on the other end of our continent."

Jeff ate it glumly, not even asking what it was stuffed with. It tasted a little like plum-stuffed spinach, odd but tolerable. He had another, afraid to talk much because he didn't want to reveal that he wasn't having the good time everyone else was. And the Grand Dragon looked so delighted with the party that he didn't want to spoil it for her.

Fargo took a large slice of what passed for holiday bread on Jamya, slathered it with iskal jam, took a bite, and beamed. "Your Dragonship, you have wonderful cooks!"

The Grand Dragon beamed. "I baked the bread myself."

Jeff thought sourly that this was typical of Fargo, who had already been told by Zi that the Grand Dragon had baked the holiday bread. Oh well, being charmingly diplomatic was one of Fargo's talents.

"Can you cook, Jeff?" asked Zargl.

"Not very well. I don't do anything very well."

"My brother is practical," Fargo said quickly, "with more common sense than most humans possess."

Jeff knew that being in a bad mood made everything seem bad, but he resented the questions and comments, slumping on his cushion so no one would notice him.

At that moment, one of the small, unintelligent worker robots threaded its way through the tables to give a folded paper to the Grand Dragon. She opened and read it.

At once, huge tears rolled down her scales onto the salad. "Mother has rejected my invitation again!"

"Oh, dear!" Zi said. "Does the Dowager give any reason?"

"Mother never gives reasons." The Grand Dragon wiped her face with the hem of her golden cape. "She never says anything. The firebees on her island simply relayed the code for 'no' to the mail rocket, which sent the message back to the computer in the Mentors' castle."

"Since this is what always happens," Zi said gently, "perhaps we should just forget about it and—"

"But my invitation made it clear that this particular party is special!" shrieked the Grand Dragon. "It's the most special party I've ever had. Not only are you humans present, but this may be the last party when all of us dragons are assembled in person. And it's not just to celebrate my birthday but to give thanks for the joy of living on Jamya, the most beautiful planet in the universe."

Jeff saw Fargo look at Albany and smile. He knew that Fargo believed only Earth deserved that label.

"Dear aunt," Zi said, "the Dowager is obviously the most dedicated of all the ruolon, and is it not the vocation of a ruolon to stay by herself in meditation, striving to gather together and use all the philosophy so hard won in her previously active life?"

The Grand Dragon sniffed. "That's just it. How can mother use any philosophy when she's isolated on the farthest island in Jamya's ocean? She is the oldest dragon of Jamya, but for fifty years none of us has received the benefit of her wisdom. She deprives us. She deprives *me!*"

"Surely your own wisdom suffices, ma'am," Fargo said.

The Grand Dragon blinked tearily, patted his hand, and gave a damp snort. "Ah, well, I just wish mother would let me know how she is. That alone would be a satisfactory birthday present. We dragons live a long time but we're not immortal. After fifty years I have the right to know if my mother is all right, and don't tell me I can trust that the firebees relayed an actual word from her."

Zi wrung her claws. "Surely the firebees are honest?"

"How do we know whether or not those on her

island have become wilder, perhaps even wicked. Oh my wings and fangs! I suspect that my mother is ill, even dead!"

"Send another message," Albany suggested.

"What's the use?" The Grand Dragon sighed smokily and collapsed back on the throne chair brought out especially for the party. Her gold cape billowed around her, her tail spines sagged, and she began crying again.

"This has definitely spoiled the party," Zargl whispered to Jeff. "The Dowager must be dead."

Jeff rose with difficulty because his legs were cramped from sitting so low down. "Your Dragonship, my robot can take me quickly to visit your mother and find out whether or not she is ill. Norby will get the coordinates of her island from the Mentors' computer and we'll leave right away."

"An excellent idea!" The Grand Dragon sat up. "I always knew that humans were intelligent. You, Jeff Wells, are also resourceful. Even if you can't persuade mother to come to my party, I will be eternally in your debt if you just find out for me how she is faring. And if the worst has happened, you and Norby must bring the— you know. Bring her back to me. Will you be able to manage that?"

"Norby will go back for the ship if necessary."

"Jeff," Fargo said, "the Grand Dragon's anxiety will be allayed sooner if Norby simply comes back here with the Dowager's body at once, and then returns to the island for you. Unless you're afraid to wait on the island alone."

"Certainly not!" Jeff said, suddenly realizing that it might not be so bad to be alone for a while. He was hardly ever alone—not at home with Fargo, or at the academy with the other cadets. And to be alone without Norby was really being alone. At first it seemed awful.

But I need it, he thought. Maybe I'll be able to yank myself out of this mood.

"I'll do my best to bring you your mother, or word from her," Jeff said, bowing to the Grand Dragon.

"Mother lives in a cave on the smallest, most northern island. Even without coordinates, Norby will find it easily from a low orbit of the planet."

"I'll get Norby right now. Perhaps we can return before the party ends."

Without waiting to hear what Fargo would say about it, Jeff ran up the marble stairs, through the palace, and out onto the front terrace, where he skidded to a stop. The Mentors' castle was quite a hike away, and he'd forgotten to ask the whereabouts of the palace communication facilities. He was so embarrassed by his own stupidity that he didn't want to go back to the party to find out. The walk would do him good but unfortunately there wasn't enough time.

Long-distance telepathy with Norby was extremely difficult and had worked only a few times before. Even the dragons and Mentors were ordinarily able to use telepathy only if they touched one another. Jeff sat on the top step of the terrace, trying to tune into Norby but unable to concentrate.

"What are you doing, Jeff? Sulking?"

"Norby! My telepathic message reached you!"

"What telepathic message?" Norby floated down

from the air over Jeff and landed with a thud on the terrace. "I came to tell you that the holov station is operating, thanks to me."

"That's good, but we don't have time to let you brag to the Grand Dragon. She wants us to visit her mother. We must go to the Mentors' castle so you can find the exact coordinates of her island from the main computer."

Norby's eyes had closed. In a minute he opened them and said, "I've got the coordinates. I beefed up the transmissions between castle and palace so I can tune in without having to go to the computer terminal. I told you I'm efficient—"

"Fine, fine. Let's go at once."

Holding Jeff's hand, Norby rose into the air until he was higher than the palace. Then he stopped.

"Why are you stopping? The view is terrific but we're in a hurry if we're going to get back to the party with either the Dowager or a message."

"Remember that the Others placed machines in orbit around Jamya that generate a force field to prevent anything leaving or entering the atmosphere of the planet in normal space. I'm calculating an entry into hyperspace that will enable us to exit on the other side of Jamya."

"You don't usually have to think about it, Norby."

"I've been exercising my cognitive circuits overtime the past few hours, trying to make a superspecial holov station for Jamya. Let's see now—here we go!"

No matter how many times Jeff had gone into the peculiar gray nothingness of hyperspace with

Norby, it always sent a trickle of fear through him, for he knew he could not survive outside Norby's protective field. Furthermore, the senses of vision and hearing did not work in hyperspace, unless one was enclosed in a ship. This meant that he and Norby could communicate only through telepathy.

—Let's get out of here, Norby. I don't like it any better than I ever did.

—I'm hurrying, Jeff. Hang on.

Brilliant sunlight stabbed at Jeff's eyes and he was momentarily blinded. Blinking, he managed to focus enough to see that they were hanging over a gigantic island. He was so confused that he couldn't tell how far up they were until he tried to focus on the trees, but got only a smudge of green. The air seemed a bit thin and smelled odd.

"What's wrong with the vegetation, Norby? And isn't this too big an island?"

"I'm sorry, Jeff. I got a little weensy bit mixed up," Norby said, sinking lower. "That's the main continent, and we're very high up." He went on sinking.

"I don't see the Mentors' castle or the palace—Norby!"

Jamya's one continent was a swampy mess, with slimy creatures like a cross between frogs and snakes writhing through the mud and weeds.

"You went back in time instead of into hyperspace!" Jeff yelled. "This is before the Others found Jamya! Before the Mentors were put here to build castles and bioengineer the dragons! It's way before the dragons even evolved! I don't see any creature higher than an amphibian."

"I'm sorry, Jeff. I'll try again. Maybe I'd better go round to the side of the planet we plan to be on when we get back to our own time. I mean up to our own time."

Norby rose again until he was so high that Jeff felt a little light-headed, and then he shot around the planet so fast that when they came to the night side, the very stars seemed to be spinning. And the stars of Jamya were not only brighter but more numerous than those of any night sky on Earth.

"I can see the other planets of this solar system quite clearly," Jeff said when Norby stopped and hung motionless near the north pole. "There's the first planet, the Sungrazer as the dragons call it. Like our Mercury, only much bigger."

"Jamya's number two and there's the third—Clouded One. But it's wrong, Jeff. It's reddish. In our time it will be fuzzy white because there's a sort of peculiar atmosphere around it, the way there is on some of the distant satellites in our solar system. Satellites of the planets like Jupiter and Saturn, I mean. I think we should investigate that planet."

"But what could have happened later to give this barren planet an atmosphere? Norby, this is very strange . . ." Jeff's voice broke off because Norby's protective field was around him. They had risen above the atmosphere of Jamya.

—No force barrier at this time, Jeff. This must be long before the Others found Jamya.

—Norby, hyperjump over to the Clouded One that isn't clouded back here. Maybe some natural phenomenon destroyed the previous atmosphere, which hasn't yet regenerated.

They dipped in and out of hyperspace so fast that Jeff wasn't prepared for the horrible sensation of falling that he had when they emerged into normal space. They were only a few kilometers from the surface of a planet that seemed to be entirely covered with reddish soil and rocks.

—No atmosphere at all, Jeff. Not even as much as Mars had before you humans put up the domes and turned it into the Martian colony. The Others must have decided Jamya was such a perfect planet that they put a force barrier around it so the newly peaceful dragons would have to stay inside it and not wander out into a dangerous solar system.

—That's right, Norby. Jamya is the only naturally habitable planet in this solar system, the way Earth is in ours. But the dragons have become content to stay on Jamya, while we humans moved out from Earth to colonize the Moon and Mars and the asteroid belt, as well as building orbital settlements like Space Command. I like being human better.

—I'm glad you like something, Jeff. That's the first positive thing I've heard you say all day. Shall I time travel up to our own time in short segments, trying to find the year when the atmosphere appears on the Clouded One?

—I wish we could, but I guess we don't have time. The Others probably toyed with making a living planet out of this dead one, but after experimenting with an atmosphere, they turned to Jamya, which already had one.

—If I found the right year, then I could try returning us to the second we left Jamya. We'd have spent only your biological time, and we could still get the Dowager Dragon—

—We can't take the chance, Norby. Much as I'd like to satisfy my curiosity, we'd better go to the Dowager Dragon.

—But I want to find out—

—Bet you can't get back to our own time right now, and bet you can't find the Dowager Dragon.

—Of course I can! I'm a genius robot! [Norby managed to sound insulted even telepathically.]

—Then prove it. You've already bollixed up this trip and if we arrive with the Grand Dragon's mother *after* the party, I can just imagine—

—I can imagine, too, Jeff. The Grand Dragon shoots a mean flame when she's annoyed.

4

In Search of the Oldest Dragon

This time the hyperjump took a little longer, but when they emerged into normal space Norby and Jeff were hanging in sunlight over a small island that had a rocky central peak with a gaping cave at the bottom, near the one tiny beach.

"This is the right time, and I'm sure it's the right place. I think I did that time-travel hyperjump perfectly."

"Yes, Norby. But how do you know whether or not this is the right island?"

"It is, it is. I came to the right coordinates and anyway I'm sure there's no other island this far north. Fortunately Jamya doesn't have ice caps like Earth. It's not quite as warm here as it is at the Grand Dragon's palace, but I think you'll find it pleasant. Shall we go down?"

"But I don't see the Dowager Dragon anywhere on the island. In fact, there seems to be only vegetation." Then Jeff remembered. "The Grand

Dragon told me that her mother was the smallest and most delicate of all the Jamyn dragons, so it's possible that she could be hidden in those trees or in the cave. Let's find out."

Norby descended to land in front of the mouth of the cave, where a little stream ran from a waterfall nearby. There was no one in sight, but a neatly weeded vegetable patch on the other side of the stream proclaimed the presence of a gardener.

"It's pleasant indeed," Jeff said, unfastening the top of his dress tunic. "Maybe nights are cooler here but the sunlight is just as warm. Look at the great vegetables. Someone who knows about gardening planted them, and I bet these clumps of flowers were planted too. I wouldn't much mind being a hermit if I could live in a place like this."

"Why doesn't she come to greet us?" asked Norby.

"She's a hermit . . . Norby, we're being stupid."

"I am not! That is—what do you mean?"

"You and I first visited Jamya long after the Dowager had retired from being Grand Dragon. If she's hiding somewhere, maybe it's because she's never seen a human before. Or a robot who looks like you. She may be very frightened by us."

"Especially since we're speaking Terran Basic."

"You're right," Jeff said, switching to Jamyn. "Hello, Madam Dowager! We've come with greetings from your daughter, the Grand Dragon of Jamya. Are you there?"

No one answered.

"We are looking for the Dowager Dragon," Jeff yelled. "Is this her island or have we made a mistake?"

From the mouth of the cave came a strange noise, remarkably like a human snore. It was accompanied by a puff of smoke that drifted toward Jeff and Norby.

"Asleep," Jeff said. "We have to remember that she's a very old lady. They sleep a lot. I hate to wake her up but time is passing and we must get back. Now the question is, can we wake her up without frightening her? She's so old she must be even more fragile. Can Jamyn dragons get heart attacks?"

"I don't know, Jeff. Never thought to ask."

"Maybe we should wait a little longer. Maybe she'll wake up of her own accord and come out of the cave."

"As you just said, we don't have time. I'll go in the cave. You know how tactful I am."

Before Jeff could disagree, Norby sailed into the cave shouting "Hey, Dowager—are you in there?"

"Norby, that's not the way to address Her ex-Dragonship!"

Swearing under his breath at cocky little robots, Jeff started toward the cave. Norby, still yelling at the top of his metallic voice, had already disappeared inside.

At the mouth of the cave Jeff was almost knocked flat by Norby's barrel hitting him in the chest.

"Hold me, Jeff. Keep me safe!"

"Keep *you* safe! You're supposed to be *my* protector."

"But you're an organic being, Jeff, and you like animals, even nasty, weird ones. You're peculiar that way. Fargo says so. You were evidently fond of animals as a small boy."

"What sort of animal is in there?"

"A horrible monster. The worst thing I've ever seen. It's got one terrible eye that was staring at me, and my sensors picked up its hot breath . . ."

"A genuine one-eyed monster like the Cyclops in the Greek myths?"

"Yes! Let's leave. I freely admit that I am not infallible. I have made a mistake. I have not brought you to the correct island."

Jeff looked at the garden again and said, "But that garden was made by an intelligent being . . . Oh, Norby! If the sea dragons have found a way to travel on land once more then it's possible that one of them has captured the Dowager Dragon!"

"And is waiting for more prey to come along. Us."

"Norby, if the monster has eaten the Dowager, we'll have to investigate. I can't go back to the Grand Dragon and say we found a monster . . ."

"Sleeping off its meal of her mother."

"You'll have to go back inside, Norby. No organic being will want to eat a metal robot."

"How do you know, Jeff? That eye was *big*. The teeth will be even bigger. Maybe the monster has one of those things inside it that Terran birds have for grinding food—"

"A crop?"

"—and will want to use my barrel in its crop instead of a rock. I don't want to go, Jeff. Let's tell the Grand Dragon we couldn't even find the island."

"I refuse to lie," Jeff said, making a fist. "I'm a

big human being and I won't be a scared child. I'm going in."

With Norby at his heels, Jeff stepped just inside the cave where the shadow began.

"I don't see a thing, Norby."

"I've taken the trouble to make a scan of the area inside this cave," Norby said pedantically, as if trying to sound calm. "There is *too* something there."

"But what?"

"I don't know."

"Maybe your sensors are wrong. Maybe you just imagined you saw something before."

"Then explain the noise we heard from the cave, Jeff."

Annoyed with himself for not paying attention to clues he'd already picked up, Jeff shouted, "Madam Dowager? Are you inside this cave?"

Suddenly the darkness in front of him changed. A slit of luminescent brightness opened and grew rounder as if it were expanding upward. As it did so, there was an increase in what Jeff realized had been an undercurrent of noise that sounded like a slow surge of ocean overlaid by a highpitched wheeze.

Jeff touched Norby.—Be prepared to go into hyperspace at my order, if this is something dangerous.

—Nothing's faster than I am. I hope.

Jeff stared at the luminescence and suddenly his stomach contracted, for he realized he was looking at an eye, the lid of which had just lifted. It was a rather large eye, looking right at him.

"Jeff, I want to go—"

The eye blinked, and a short distance away from it in the darkness, another slit opened. Soon two huge eyes stared at Jeff and Norby.

There was a loud scraping crash, as if an enormous tail had slapped down on rocks much further back in the cave. Then something bulky stirred in the darkness.

Jeff backed away from it until he was standing at the mouth of the cave.

"I think we should leave now, Jeff," Norby said in Terran Basic.

"Wait," Jeff answered in the same language. "We must find out if it's captured the Dowager."

"It doesn't seem likely that a monster is going to be particularly informative about what it's had for dinner. Sometimes your curiosity gets us into more trouble than anything I ever do. I suggest that we go back to the main continent and tell the Grand Dragon."

"Tell her that we didn't really try to find out if her mother was eaten by a monster in a cave? No, Norby. We'll get information first. Besides, the monster isn't lunging at us. Perhaps it'll go back to sleep—"

An ominous rumbling filled the cave, followed by a loud scraping as if gigantic claws were unsheathed and being sharpened on rock.

"What have you done with the Dowager Dragon?" Jeff yelled, forgetting to return to the Jamyn language.

Out of the deepest shadow of the cave moved a large creature, dark and rumbling to itself. As Norby tried to pull him back, Jeff watched the creature lumber forward until it reached the faint shadow in the front of the cave.

"Jeff, look at those wild eyes and the size of those fangs! The whole thing is almost as big as the civilized dragons' ancestors. I tell you it must be a sea dragon, and therefore primitive and dangerous." He tugged at Jeff's tunic. "I want to leave right away!"

"How can it be a sea dragon when it has arms and legs? Land animals that return to the sea to live for generations usually evolve flippers or something practical to swim with."

"I don't think a scientific discussion is in order here, Jeff, especially since this monster is opening its mouth and if it flames right at me my innards might get cooked!"

"You can always zoom away on antigrav or enter hyperspace to save yourself. I think you should now shoot past the creature and see if you can find the Dowager in the back of the cave, or any bones that might be hers."

"Are you going to distract this critter so it won't weld my circuits?"

"I'll try." Jeff backed further out of the cave. "Do you think if I waved my arms like this—"

But before Norby could comment, the monster threw back its head with a terrible hiss, immediately followed by a deafening roar as a gigantic flame shot out of the very toothy mouth.

Jeff, stumbling backward to get out of the way, fell over Norby and landed on hard rock. Norby clutched his arm.

"Let's leave, Jeff! It might not miss us next time."

"Something's different, Norby."

At first Jeff couldn't figure it out, but then he realized that the cave was not as dark as before and he could see the large scaly body of the monster better. He craned his neck but still couldn't tell if one of the little Jamyn dragons was alive or dead at the back of the cave.

"There's a flame from that rock, Jeff! The monster has set the place on fire!"

"That's impossible. You can't set a rock on fire."

"Look!"

At first Jeff thought that the monster itself was flaming continuously, but then he saw that Norby was right. A flame jetted from the top of a hunk of stone resting on a ledge inside the cave.

In the flickering light, Jeff could see the monster much more clearly. It was fully twice as large as any Jamyn dragon, with ragged green scales, blunted tail spikes, and a missing point on one of its long fangs. The points of the other fangs were still quite sharp enough for anything the monster wished to do with them.

Jeff slowly rose to his feet and tried backing away again.

"I don't think I'll look for the Dowager's body just yet," Norby said, still clutching Jeff.

"Maybe later," Jeff said. "Maybe after the monster goes for a swim or whatever. We could watch from the top of a tree—"

"Look out, Jeff!"

The monster's head was up again, the mouth open. Smoke belched out and Jeff, getting a lungful, coughed.

"Who?"

The monster roared out the question, along with

a burst of flame and considerably more smoke.

Jeff tried to answer but his eyes were watering and he could only cough.

"Who!" The word was said in flawless Jamyn.

5

Persuasion

Norby was pulling on Jeff's arm. "Why don't you give me the order to take you away from here, Jeff? I don't like—"

"Hush, Norby. We must speak in Jamyn from now on."

"Did the monster ask 'who' or was it someone at the back of the cave?"

"I don't know." Jeff switched to Jamyn. "I am a human from planet Earth. My name is Jeff Wells and this is my personal teaching robot, Norby."

The fire burning from the hunk of stone wobbled and went out. Before Jeff's eyes could readapt to the darkness inside the cave, the creature's body moved quickly. He saw the great luminescent eyes flash and then there was another roar.

Jeff winced, waiting to feel burned, but all that happened was that flame sprang from the stone once more, burning brightly. It was an old-fashioned oil lamp, newly relit.

He saw now that the monster's spiky tail and the sharp foreclaws were held high, as if ready to slash down at victims.

"Madam Dowager, your highness—"

"Humph!" There was a smoky snort. "You might at least bow in the presence of ex-royalty, even if you are a most peculiar and unattractive alien monster."

Jeff quickly bowed. "I am honored to meet you, Your Dragonness."

"Most awesome and mighty Dragonness," Norby added in a particularly tinny voice.

"Jeff Wells, from planet Earth?" She bent forward to sniff at Jeff. "Never heard of the place. Are all the sentient creatures there the same peculiar shape and color you are?"

"We're of similar shapes, in several colors. We applaud our diversity—"

"Ugh! I am not interested in aliens. Go away."

"But ma'am, we've come to visit you because—"

"It's outrageous!" the oldest dragon said, puffing another cloud of smoke at Jeff that made him cough. "I thought that going to the farthest and coldest island on Jamya would ensure my privacy but after only fifty years of retirement I'm intruded upon like this, and by alien monsters!"

"But if no one has visited you for fifty years, surely you've read the letters sent to you—"

"I am in meditative retirement, you idiot!"

"Then you don't know anything about humans, or even that the Mentor robots are alive and helping the dragons now?"

"Bah! I am not interested! Go away, alien monster, and take that sawed-off version of a robot with you."

"I am a perfect size and shape!" Norby yelled back.

Jeff slapped a hand on Norby's hat to establish telepathic contact.—Please don't say or do anything to make her more annoyed, Norby. We have to persuade her to come with us.

—I don't want to persuade her. She's mean and nasty and too big for me to put both of you inside my protective field since we'll have to go back in a hurry, through hyperspace.

—You'll take her and then come back for me.

—I'm not taking that creature anywhere! She'd probably decide she didn't like the trip and melt me down.

—I'm sure you're more or less fireproof.

—It's the 'less' that bothers me, Jeff.

—Shut, up, Norby. She's beginning to smoke again.

"Have you been struck dumb, human named Jeff? What is the matter with you? Why don't you just leave?"

"I was instructing my robot. We do it telepathically."

"Jamya doesn't need another telepathic species."

"Humans aren't ordinarily telepathic. I am because your granddaughter Zi made it possible."

"Zi actually risked contamination by biting an alien monster to transfer the telepathic talent?" The dragon's heavy eyelids raised until she was staring fiercely at Jeff. "What did you do to persuade her—threats? Bodily harm?"

"No, ma'am. She wanted me to be able to understand her. It was quite a while ago. We're good friends now, and I know your daughter, the Grand Dragon, well. That's why—we came."

"Go away. I know nothing about Jamya as it is today and I do not wish to know."

"But it's been fifty years—"

"A short time for meditating in one's old age."

"And your daughter is afraid that something has happened to you because you haven't sent any word except 'no' . . ."

The dragon touched the purple disk hanging from her gold antigrav collar. "I told my firebees to answer 'no' to any request coming by mail rocket. Go back to the palace and inform my daughter that I'm as well as can be expected. Even if I were dying the monitor pendant wouldn't let anyone know because I had it adjusted. I'm old and I have a right to die when I choose. After I am thoroughly dead the monitor will notify my relatives."

"You couldn't be that good a hermit if you talk to your firebees," Norby said. "Maybe nobody can be really alone."

The dragon sat back on her haunches, rolling her eyes upward. "It's a pity I've taken a vow of pacifism. It would be such pleasure, such a relief to burn up this persistent organic monster and his revolting robot."

"You're revolting!" Norby shouted. "You don't care about anyone but yourself! You just want to do what you want to do and you're not willing to help anyone!"

"Norby!" Jeff said. "Control your emotive circuits!"

"Furthermore," Norby continued, "You not only talk to the firebees—and I sense that there's a whole cloud of them hanging in the back of your cave—but I bet you've established some form of communication with the sea dragons. Out of my back eyes I can see down to the beach and there are three of them half out of the water, perhaps trying to hear us."

The dragon blinked, and sighed.

"Is it true, ma'am?" Jeff asked. "You talk to the bees and the sea dragons?"

"They're not exactly good conversationalists, but I've established moderately friendly relationships so that the bees don't sting me and the sea dragons don't nip at my tail when I bathe. Tell me, human, are you and that talkative robot of yours planning to stay on this island? I will ask the sea dragons to help me move to another island. My antigrav collar still works but I'm a bit old for heavy-duty flying."

"We're not staying, ma'am. We came only to ask you to return with us briefly to the palace, for your daughter's birthday party. She's very sad that you aren't there."

"It's extravagant, vain, and foolish of my daughter to keep up the royal birthday tradition."

"Then I guess we'll go," Jeff said, taking Norby's hand. "Goodbye, Your Dragonness . . ."

The dragon cleared her throat and said softly, "Um—before you leave, you might at least explain what kind of creature a human is."

—She's curious, Jeff. Play on that.

—Perhaps you can help, Norby. Touch her—

—I don't want to!

—You must. Touch and open your data banks on Jamya to her mind. Then she'll know everything that's happened, and all about us. "Ma'am," Jeff said aloud, "my robot wishes to transfer information to you."

"Will it hurt?"

"I never hurt anybody! I know the laws of robotics!"

The dragon sighed again. "I suppose if you leave without informing me, I will always wonder who you are and it will disturb my meditation. Go ahead, Norby. Touch me."

Norby stretched out his extensible arm to its full length and touched the very tip of the dragon's tail, now coiled in front of her. He shut all his eyes, and she shut hers. They were both still and silent for a couple of minutes.

"Well!" said the dragon. "Well, well! So you and the Mentor robots have constructed such a high-tech holov station that from now on there won't be any major assemblage of us dragons. Every meeting will take place holographically. I think that is to be deplored."

"Not if dragons prefer being alone," Jeff said slyly.

"Solitary meditation is an achievement of old age. At least it's supposed to be," she finished lamely, looking at the firebees and the sea dragons.

"Many hermits in the history of Earth have, after years of meditating alone, returned to the world they once knew in order to teach, to pass on what they have learned."

"I'm not sure I've learned anything," the Dowager said softly and sadly. "Not enough. I wish I had. I would like to be of use—not the way I was when I ruled Jamya as Grand Dragon. No, I've finished with that. But there must be something—*something* that will give my life a sort of completion."

"You can start by making your daughter happy on her birthday," Jeff said. "Please come to the party. We have just enough time to get there before it's too late. And your greatgranddaughter Zargl, Zi's daughter, will enjoy meeting you."

"I'm glad Zi has budded," the Dowager said. "I raised Zi after her mother, my second daughter, was killed when her antigrav collar came unfastened and fell off while she was flying over the ocean. The sea dragons ate her. Zi has been afraid of the ocean ever since, but I am not. At my age one fears nothing, except uselessness."

"Jeff, I don't think we ought to try taking the Dowager back to the palace without a ship," Norby said. "I'll go get the *Hopeful*."

"Then you'll go to the party, ma'am?" Jeff asked.

"Yes, I'll go. Mainly because it's to be the last."

"Hurry, Norby. I'll stay here." Jeff said, touching Norby once more.—And so she won't change her mind.

—Okay, Jeff. Be right back.

When Norby vanished, the Dowager's tail twitched, but then she smiled at Jeff, showing all her fangs. "Come, I wish to bathe before the party."

"But there isn't time—"

"There is always time for the right things." She stomped past Jeff, out of the cave, and down to the sandy beach, plunging into the water with her leathery wings flapping.

The sea dragons had slid back at the Dowager's approach, and Jeff followed to the water line, wondering how he could possibly save her if these sea dragons were not as friendly as she thought. They had narrow flat heads with little cranial capacity, and their upper two fangs were permanently on view, pointing outward.

"Be careful, Your Dragonness!"

"Remove your garments and join me, young human. The water is fine and one always bathes before meeting the Grand Dragon."

"I had a shower this morning, ma'am." But he took off his boots and socks, put them on the nearest flat rock, and let his toes curl in and out of the sand.

"I've told the sea dragons to bring me the jelly eggs of one of the lowlier creatures on the ocean floor. My daughter is fond of them and they'll be my birthday present to her."

"I hope it won't take long for them to bring the eggs. The *Hopeful* has just appeared overhead." Jeff was relieved. Norby had been incredibly efficient.

"I believe the sea dragon messenger is coming now," the Dowager said. "Perhaps you should step back—"

It was too late. With a boisterous roar, a huge sea dragon reared up, remarkably resembling ancient Terran drawings of the mythical sea serpent, although this one seemed to have tentacles as well as clawed flippers. It threw a package of wet, slimy eggs, loosely encased in seaweed netting, smack onto Jeff's boots and socks.

The boots were easily wiped off but the socks were hopeless. As Jeff helped the Dowager—and the present of eggs—into the *Hopeful*, he was conscious of the fact that Norby had undoubtedly seen the whole thing.

"You're lucky, human Jeff," the Dowager said, once they were inside the ship. "That was the worst of the sea dragons. It has not only an unpleasant sense of humor but an insatiable hunger. I sensed that it was actually planning to eat you, but since it fears me, it merely did the job of delivering the eggs in a way that would bother you."

"Have you always had power over animals, ma'am?"

"Some, perhaps, along with talents for . . ."

"For what?" Jeff asked.

"You have an extraordinary amount of curiosity, young human, don't you?"

"I'm sorry. My older brother Fargo laughs at me for it. And I am curious about your talents."

"I used to think I had a talent for persuasion," the Dowager said, tapping the odd little hairs growing out of the end of her scaly chin. "At least with firebees and sea dragons. I certainly failed at persuading you to leave me alone. It was you who persuaded me to go back to the palace, in spite of the fear I sensed that you felt for me. Are you a particularly brave human, Jeff Wells?"

"No. But I do like the Grand Dragon a lot, and I'd hate to return without you and disappoint her.

She wants to see her mother again, and I'm sure the rest of the dragons will be interested to hear about your talents for persuading the animals in your vicinity—"

"Stop flattering me, human. If I've learned one thing in my meditation, it's never to take things as they seem, but only as they are."

"I wasn't flattering you. I thought I spoke truthfully."

"Jeff Wells, don't romanticize my supposed talents, for there is only one thing I genuinely have."

"What's that, ma'am?"

"Age. That is usually mysterious to someone young." The dragon laughed. "It's even mysterious to the old, too."

At the control board, Norby said, "We'll be over the palace soon." He touched Jeff to establish telepathic contact.—Be careful, Jeff. I don't trust this dragon. Do they all grow that big with age or is she special?

—I don't know, Norby, but I suppose the Jamyn dragons are like many Terran reptiles that keep growing as long as they live.

—Well, if her persuasive powers have grown, it's too bad she wasn't around when you were packing, to make you put in enough extra pairs of socks.

6

THE WEATHER CHANGES

Warm and dry in his spare pair of socks, Jeff basked in praise from the Grand Dragon. She'd almost fainted when her mother descended from the *Hopeful*, but now her relief and delight overflowed onto the heroes of the day, Jeff and—it seemed—especially Norby.

The little robot was telling the story in suitably heroic tones. "And I had to rescue Jeff and the Dowager dragon from vicious sea dragons, too . . ."

"It wasn't exactly like that, Norby," Jeff began.

"Eat your dessert, Jeff," Norby scolded. "You're a growing boy."

"If he grows any more there won't be a dress uniform that will fit him," Fargo said.

"I think he looks cute with his wrists hanging out like that," Zargl said, snuggling up to Jeff. "I'm so happy you made it possible for me to meet my great-grandmother."

"Norby made it possible," Jeff said before Norby could.

"This is the best birthday I have ever had," said the Grand Dragon, engulfing another slice of the birthday pie. Jamyn dragons always celebrate with pie, not cake, and the Grand Dragon's favorite was made from a vegetable somewhat like Terran pumpkins. Jeff thought the dessert too highly spiced, but Fargo obviously relished it.

"Fargo," Norby said sternly, "if *you* have another slice of birthday pie, it won't be your *wrists* that will look too large for your uniform."

Fargo grunted. "You've been acting like Jeff's nursemaid, Norby. Don't extend the act to include me. And why are you doing it in the first place?"

"I'm planning a book on the care and feeding of humans. I'll start it as soon as my Great Federation Novel is accepted by the publishers. They must be reading and rereading it, trying to decide what fabulous sum to pay me . . ."

"I wouldn't bet on that, Norby," Fargo said bitterly, since his own Great Federation Novel had been rejected. "Albany, my love, do you think I'm too fat for more pie?"

She slid one hand under his tunic and gave him the pinch test. "As skinny—excuse me— svelte as ever. More pie is clearly indicated, especially since we won't be able to bake it at home—the spices don't grow in our part of the galaxy."

"I always knew there was some reason I'm crazy about you, Albany. You appreciate my finer points."

"Hah!" said Albany.

Jeff, listening to all this, began to feel lonely again. One of these days Fargo would marry Albany, and in the meantime Jeff had so much growing up to do—finishing at Space Academy, finding a job or a position in Space Command, finding a wife—if a certain young princess on a far-away planet didn't snare him first. He sighed and looked up at the starry sky, so open and so free of all the uncomfortable emotions of human life.

Jeff and Norby had missed most of the birth-day program. The younger dragons had already given one exhibition of antigrav dancing, which Albany—with a decided twinkle in her eyes— said had to be seen to be believed. He'd also missed a whole series of speeches, toasts, and even Fargo's song.

"I was a hit," Fargo said.

"Courtesy of Gilbert and Sullivan." Albany kissed the frown that immediately corrugated Fargo's head and she added, "But I love you even if you are a plagiarist. Fortunately G and S have been in the public domain for a few years—"

"A few hundred!"

"And you are the last of the great minstrels, darling, so I am smitten." Albany smiled at him and began to sing. " 'None shall part us from each other—' "

" 'One in life and death are we—' "

The dragons at the table stopped talking and listened to the two human lovers sing the famous duet from *Iolanthe*, but Jeff grinned when Albany deliberately avoided singing what the submissive Victorian female was supposed to sing to the male. Instead, *she* sang "I the ocean, thou the billow; I the sunrise, thou the day!" Fargo shrugged and gently bit each of her fingertips.

The Dowager was eye-catching, for she was the oldest, by far the largest dragon present, and the only one not wearing an elaborate robe and as many jewels as would fit. She sat on her haunches at the main table like a huge green monolith, smiling occasionally, but Jeff had the feeling that she knew she no longer belonged to Jamyn society.

Mentor First had been particularly polite to the Dowager. In her day, Jamya was a much simpler place, with the Mentor robots all but inactivated in their castle, and no humans coming to visit. The Dowager had been equally polite to Mentor First, but made no attempt to be genuinely friendly to the big robot, or indeed to anyone. As the festivities went on, and it grew later and later, she stifled a great yawn and tapped Jeff on the shoulder. When he turned, she whispered into his ear.

"I want to go back to my island, human Jeff Wells. I am not used to such crowds, noise, and confusion. And rich food. Please ask your little robot to take me home in your ship."

"I will, Ma'am."

"As soon as Norby finishes talking," she added.

Norby was at the moment explaining how he and Mentor First had put the new holov station into operation and that even now, the birthday party was being broadcast to any dragon unable to attend in person.

"It's a powerful station," Mentor First added. "I don't completely understand what Norby did, but I believe that from now on anyone watching it will have the experience of feeling as if she is actually in whatever scene is shown."

"What did you do, Norby?" Albany asked. She understood machinery and electronics considerably better than Fargo.

"Well, I sort of, that is—I'm not cer—it's a trade secret."

"The trade of necromancers?" Fargo winked at Albany. "Or did you merely exorcise the evil influences . . ."

"Don't make fun of me," Norby said. "I'm a genius robot and now Jamya has a perfect holov station."

Jeff tried to attract Norby's attention so he could tell him quietly that the Dowager wanted to go home, but Norby kept on talking. Bored, Jeff looked up to study the brilliant night sky of Jamya.

A bank of cloud was slowly creeping across the sky, and one by one the stars were winking out as it blocked the way for their light to reach Jamya.

"Oh, blast!" Jeff said aloud, without thinking. "I think it's going to rain."

"It can't rain," the Grand Dragon said. "We had rain day before yesterday and it's not due to rain again for a week."

"There do seem to be heavy clouds overhead," Albany said. "I can't see the stars anymore."

Mentor First stood motionless, staring upward. "I am scanning the sky. Norby, confirm my readings. Is not that cloud remarkably high up? It seems to be at the very top of the planet's atmosphere. Rain clouds do not do that."

"You're right, father. And I think it's not an ordinary rain cloud, although it's hard to tell what kind of rain cloud it is because my sensors are having trouble penetrating it and analyzing it. Yours too, father?"

"Yes. This may be an unusual weather pattern that has not recurred for many years."

"I've never seen it before," the Dowager said.

"It may antedate the coming of the Others," Mentor First said, "but I will return to the castle and ask the main computer if there's any record . . ."

"I've just asked it," Norby said. "Nothing like this has shown up in any weather pattern on record."

"Then perhaps it won't really rain," the Grand Dragon said with a hopeful smile. "And my party won't be spoiled."

"I don't like it," Norby said.

7

No Protection

The dragons were whispering among themselves, as if afraid to talk out loud, and all kept looking up at the sky.

"I don't understand why a cloud is such a frightening thing," Albany said. "On Earth we have such violent weather I suppose we're used to the possibility of an outdoor party getting rained on. Surely a cloud is a cloud, regardless of how high up it is."

"Listen!" Norby yelled, rising into the air on antigrav until he was higher than anyone's head and commanded attention. "I've just tuned in to the main computer again. According to data received from scanners located all over the planet, that mysterious cloud now encircles Jamya."

"At the equator?" Fargo asked.

"Excuse me," Norby said. " 'Encircles' was the wrong word. The cloud completely envelops the entire planet. On the present day side of Jamya, sunlight has been sufficiently blocked so that it seems like dusk."

"That's impossible!" The Grand Dragon shook her fist at the sky as if intending to punish it. "No cloud can totally cover a planet."

"Venus, a planet in our solar system, is totally clouded up," Jeff said, "but that's differ—Norby! Where are you going! Come back!"

Norby had shot upward, fast. His words came back in the increasingly chilly night air. "I'm going up for a look, and a closer scan."

Jeff pulled at his brother. "Fargo, let's go to the *Hopeful* and follow him! It might be dangerous—"

"But Norby is right," Mentor First said. "We must have more information about this cloud, and his scanners will provide it from close range."

Jeff dug his fingers into his palms, trying not to yell, for Fargo had nodded to Mentor First and clamped a hand on Jeff's shoulder to keep him from leaving.

—Whatever this cloud is, Jeff, Norby should be okay. He's done the only intelligent thing.

—He should have taken me with him!

—He tries to protect you, little brother.

—Stop calling me that! I'm sick of being thought of as a child! When Norby goes into danger, I want to go too!

Jeff brushed off Fargo's hand, breaking the telepathic contact, and searched the sky for a glimpse of Norby, who was by then too far away to see. Many minutes passed, and Jeff was almost afraid to breathe.

The Dowager suddenly rose to full height. "The

small robot is coming back. And something is wrong."

At first it looked as if Norby were falling out of control, but at the last moment his antigrav seemed to turn on and he landed heavily next to Mentor First. He was completely closed up, with even his sensor wire withdrawn.

"Norby," Mentor First said gently, touching him with his lower pair of hands. "Are you all right?"

Jeff scrambled over to Norby and picked him up, trying to make telepathic contact. There was no response.

"He can't be dead!" Jeff said wildly. "He turned on his antigrav, so he's alive in there somewhere. Why doesn't he talk to me! Norby! Norby!"

Norby's head slowly emerged from his barrel, his eyes shut. "Don't yell, Jeff. I have the robot equivalent of a bad headache." The front pair of eyes opened. "I'm intact, but just barely."

"What is the cloud?" Mentor First asked.

"A mess of organic and inorganic molecules that's not safe for anyone to be around. Certainly not any of you organics, human or dragon, and I fear that in spite of my protective field the gases and electronic pulsations might eventually deactivate my robot brain."

"Is the cloud alive?" the Dowager Dragon asked. It was such an appalling question that everyone turned to stare at her.

"Is it *what*?" Norby blinked at her.

"Is it possible that the entire planet-covering cloud is something that moved here from somewhere else? Can it be an alien entity? Alive?"

"I hadn't considered that," Norby said, after

a moment's thought. "It wasn't evident in any data I picked up in what scanning I was able to do without going into the cloud itself. It was dangerous just being near it."

"But you're thinking of the cloud as an 'it'— as an entity?" The Dowager smiled toothily at Norby. "I suspect that with your emotive circuits, you are a robot capable of intuition. What does your intuition tell you, irrespective of the data from your scanners?"

"I think it's an entity that used to be around the third planet, the one you dragons call the 'Clouded One.'" Norby explained to the dragons what he and Jeff had seen when they went back in time—a third planet devoid of atmosphere.

"If this cloud thing has moved from the third planet to the second, it will destroy life on Jamya just by cutting off the sunlight," cried the Grand Dragon.

The fear in everyone's mind had been spoken. Jeff remembered the theory that when clouds of dust from collisions and volcanic explosions covered Earth sixty-five million years ago, there were enough years of only dim sunlight to kill off the great dinosaurs. This strange cloud was blocking more sunlight than that.

"And furthermore," said the Grand Dragon in outraged tones, "why hasn't our force field barrier protected us from this invasion? The Others put it there for our protection."

"It's gone," Norby said. "The main computer's scanners indicate that just before the cloud settled around the planet, it deactivated all the orbital generators that produce Jamya's barrier field.

That's how the cloud was able to get into the top of the atmosphere."

"Jamya—open to invasion from space!" The Grand Dragon held a claw over her eyes.

"Hardly, my daughter," said the Dowager. "We may not have a force field barrier now, but we have a new barrier, much more dangerous. And if it moved here purposefully, then it is an entity, and alive. I propose communicating with it."

"I have been trying," Norby said. "Nothing happens."

The Dowager's tail smote the ground and everyone stopped talking. "Dragons of Jamya! Robots! Human guests! A strange cloudlike entity from normal space has surrounded our planet. If it moves closer to the surface of Jamya it will destroy us quickly. If it stays where it is, life on Jamya will eventually die out."

"My robot can move ships through hyperspace, ma'am," Jeff said. "With our ship we can evacuate your people one group at a time. You don't need to die."

"Young human, our *home* will die, and all the other creatures on it will not be evacuated and they will die." She pointed to the firebees, winking among the flowers. "Besides, where would you take us Jamyn dragons? Any planet suitable for our life will also have other life forms on it."

"There aren't that many of you," Fargo said. "Earth would find room."

—I can imagine the politicians on Earth arguing about where to put several thousand dragons [Norby said to Jeff].

"Thank you, kind human, but I prefer to do

something about this situation. I have developed skills in communicating with animal minds. I must go to this cloud and find out if it has a mind, and what it wants."

"It's probably mindless," Mentor First said. "There's no indication from Norby's scanning that it is anything but a vast entity of alien matter that has moved from one planet to another."

"But *why* did it move?" asked the Grand Dragon.

Norby's head sank into his barrel most of the way. "Maybe I made the holov too strong, and instead of bouncing off the satellites that generated the barrier field, the holov signals went on through and hit the third planet."

"Yes," said the Dowager, scratching her chin, "and attracted a creature composed of gas and energy that probably also eats energy—the way it ate the force field. You didn't know this would happen so you needn't feel guilty, little robot. Don't worry, since Jamya is in grave danger, it is up to *me*—the oldest dragon—to visit this cloud. I will go in the ship that brought me to the party, if someone will be the pilot."

"No, mother!" The Grand Dragon shouted. "I must go."

"The only Jamyn to go will be me," said the Dowager.

"I order you to stay here, and I am Grand Dragon! All Jamyn dragons must obey my orders!"

"Except that all Jamyn dragons must obey their mothers," the Dowager Dragon said, patting the Grand Dragon on her top head spike. "I'm still your mother. I will go."

"And I will take you, ma'am," Fargo said, springing to his feet and bowing low. "I can pilot the ship. I also enjoy danger, and I will protect you."

"Well, I hardly think we're going to do battle," the Dowager said. "The point is to be safely inside a ship, able to scan the cloud at leisure and relay the data to the main computer. I will also be close enough to find out if the cloud is indeed mindless. I accept your offer, Fargo Wells."

"I must go with you," Norby said.

"No, little robot. You must be kept safely on the planet, to come to our aid in an emergency. Am I right, Mentor First, in thinking that within a ship we organics will not be damaged by the cloud's gases, but that the electronic vibrations might still damage you robots?"

"That is so, Madam Dowager, but the cloud may inactivate the ship's computer too."

"I can pilot the ship manually," Fargo said. "The Dowager Dragon can still get a close look at the cloud."

"I want to go along," Jeff said.

"No, I will." Albany's face was grim. "This is a police matter. The cloud has disrupted our party and blocked our sunlight. It is criminal . . ."

"I won't have you along, taking risks, Albany," Fargo said. "And on further reflection, I've decided to go alone, Madam Dowager. I'll come back and report—"

The Dowager loomed over Fargo, brandishing a mighty claw. "I could break you in half, human. You'll take me or else."

"Well, if you insist."

"Fargo!" Albany started to argue.

"No, love. We'll keep in touch by ship's communication." Fargo kissed her, and waved at Jeff.

The Grand Dragon ran up to her mother. "I've waited fifty years to say hello to you again and now you're going into what may be terrible danger. I want to say that I love you."

The Dowager snorted, but her eyes became suspiciously moist and she clutched her daughter to her scaly front. "I'm proud of you, dear. You've taken good care of Jamya since I retired. Everything looks beautiful and so do you, except for the excess weight."

"I'll go on a diet. I promise."

"And I do think it's time for you to bud. Every Grand Dragon needs an heir."

"I'm sorry, mother, but I'm not able to bud. Some of us can't, you know. I've decided on a young dragon as my heir, someone experienced in observing and dealing with humans and other strange aspects of our universe. (At these words Zargl blushed a darker green.) We can't stay closed in on Jamya forever."

"I'm not sure I approve, although it may be an academic matter since the cloud . . . but perhaps, if all goes well, you will be right. I will help, if I can." The Dowager's voice dropped, and she sighed. "I haven't been much help to you all these years I've been trying to meditate. I don't have much more time to find out how I can be useful."

"Are you ill, mother? The Mentors can treat you—"

"I am quite certain that no treatment will be efficacious but do not worry. I won't be dying quickly"—she looked up at the cloud—"at least I hope not, although that is one solution to the illnesses of old age."

The Grand Dragon began to sob and her mother patted her. "Be brave, daughter." The Dowager turned and opened her great leathery wings. She rose into the air, plucked Fargo out of the embrace of Albany as if he weighed nothing, and flew to the *Hopeful*.

A lump in his throat, Jeff waved goodbye as the small ship rose into the atmosphere, higher and higher until it was out of sight.

8

INTO THE Cloud

A sad and worried population of dragons waited for news about the fate of their planet, while Jeff, Albany, and Norby went to the Mentors' castle with the Grand Dragon. It was getting late, but no one suggested returning to the palace for any sleep. Norby and Mentor First tuned the main computer to the *Hopeful*'s wavelength.

"Hiya, everybody," Fargo said. His image was distorted, and becoming more so the further into the cloud the ship went.

"Your image isn't coming through, Fargo," Mentor First said. "The cloud is distorting that part of the communication but your voice is still clear. I will turn off the visual."

"I'm still my handsome self and the Dowager Dragon is as magnificently royal as ever."

"Bah!" The Dowager sounded as if she were grinding her fangs. "I'm antique royalty, but even an antique would prefer a ship with more room in it."

"Just put your tail in that direction, ma'am," Fargo said soothingly. "Then it won't be as cramped."

"I am relieved that your ship's computer is still functioning," Mentor First said.

"It's fine."

"That's because it's a very stupid computer," Norby said. "Perhaps the energy of the cloud only affects intelligent beings, like me."

"Did you remember to put your personal shield on when you were up here, Norby?" Fargo asked.

"Yes, after I began to sense the effects."

"That must have helped," Fargo said. "Perhaps the hull of the ship is a good enough shield for this computer. It certainly keeps us organics safe. I feel fine."

"I also," said the Dowager.

"But what do you see up there?" asked Jeff.

"Thick fog, resembling the proverbial pea soup. I'm transmitting the scanning to the main Jamyn computer. Are you receiving the data?"

Norby's sensor wire was plugged into the computer so he said, "Data coming in, Fargo. That stuff you're in may look like fog, but it is very different. It is a peculiar form of matter with an even more peculiar energy pattern. The computer doesn't know anything about such an entity and my data bank sure doesn't either. It's probably as lethal to organic beings as it would be to robots, but fortunately it's outside."

"If a ship's shielding is so effective, I will prepare my own ship and join you," Mentor First said.

"With me," Norby said.

"And me!" Albany and Jeff added simultaneously.

"No!" Fargo yelled. "Give me time to study this foggy stuff and see what's what. The Dowager hasn't had a chance to find out if the thing has any intelligence at all."

"I will have to go outside the ship," the Dowager said.

"You can't do that without a space suit and there's none aboard that will fit you!" Fargo sounded exasperated, as if the Dowager had been stubborn all the way up to the cloud.

"Then I will go into the airlock, so that only the outside door will be between me and the cloud. Perhaps there I'll be able to detect whether or not the energy patterns outside the ship are a sign of intelligence."

"Now wait . . ." Fargo began.

"Mother, don't do that!" shouted the Grand Dragon.

Mentor First held up one of his upper hands. "It is probable that there will be no physical danger to Her Dragonness inside the airlock. Perhaps she should try to communicate with the cloud. If she fails to do so, we will assume it is not an intelligent entity."

"Your Dragonness, there's a microphone in the airlock," Norby said. "You will be able to talk to the ship's computer, which will broadcast your words to Fargo and also to us."

"Then it's settled," the Dowager said. "I'm going into the airlock now."

"I'll help you in, ma'am," Fargo said, in the voice

he used when being gallant to females.

There was silence for a few minutes until Fargo's voice returned. "The Dowager is safe inside the airlock now. I'm going back to the control room to monitor the computer."

"Blast!" Jeff yelled. "Why didn't you take me with you! I could have watched the airlock in case the Dowager Dragon needed help."

"Thank you, human Jeff Wells," the Dowager said, "I understand the need to be useful, but I assure you that help is not needed. I am somewhat cramped but otherwise comfortable and safe. I will now turn off the incoming speaker so that I may meditate in silence, attempting to discover whether or not the cloud is indeed an entity and if so, one with a mind."

"Leave the microphone on!" yelled Fargo.

"Certainly," the Dowager said, a slight edge in her voice. "I may be ancient and out of date, but I am not stupid. How else would you know when I wish to leave the airlock for the rather dubious comfort of your ship?"

"Well yes, ma'am, but—" Fargo paused. "She can't hear me now. Oh, well, I think I'll play my guitar, since it's unlikely that anything interesting is going to happen. That cloud is probably just a weird natural phenomenon and maybe if a certain too-inventive robot named Norby turns off the holov station the cloud will move back to planet three."

Jeff could hear Fargo tuning his guitar, while Norby rushed to turn off the holov broadcast, maintaining only the ship to planet communication.

"Fargo is right. We should have turned it off hours ago," Mentor First said.

"If the cloud is the one from the third planet," Norby said, "it moved very quickly to Jamya, for I hadn't had the holov going for many hours. I'll calculate how many hours before it should move away after we deprive it of the holov energy."

The Grand Dragon gulped. "What if it likes Jamya better than the third planet, even with the holov off? What if . . ."

"Let's wait," Albany said. "Count the hours, Norby."

"Approximately three. Do you realize what that means?"

"That we only have to wait three hours for it to move," Mentor First said.

"No, sir," Jeff said, frightened. "It means that to move that quickly from the third planet to the second, the cloud had to go faster than light. The cloud has the capacity to move through hyperspace."

"Then it could have hyperjumped over the barrier field around Jamya," Fargo said. "It didn't because it must have wanted to eat the energy of the field, and it knocked out the field generators in the process."

There was an exceptionally long pause, during which no one spoke and everyone thought about the powers of the alien cloud.

"I'm so worried," the Grand Dragon finally said. "Mother, I think you and Fargo should return to Jamya."

"She can't hear you," Fargo said. "In a little while, I'll go knock on the airlock, but in the meantime, we seem to be perfectly safe in the ship and while the Dowager's doing her thing and the computer's doing its—and the Mentors' computer is analyzing everything—I'm going to sing my song, because Jeff hasn't heard it. Here goes."

There was the sound of throat clearing, then vibrating strings as Fargo plucked out a rippling arpeggio.

"Of all the Grand Dragons there've been, This present Grand Dragon's the finest— Her royalty's never been dim . . ."

The Grand Dragon interrupted. "The song is all very well, even if it doesn't exactly rhyme, but I assure you that my mother was the most elegant Grand Dragon in the history of Jamya. Fargo, I do wish you'd get her out of the airlock now."

"On my way," Fargo said. Jeff could hear the faint musical vibration as Fargo put down his guitar. "My music was giving me a headache anyway. Funny, it never did that before."

"Fargo, are you sure you're all right?" Jeff asked.

"I'm not in the pink but—"

A tremendous roar had interrupted Fargo. When the noise stopped, Jeff could hear the sound of running feet.

"I trust you folks down below heard the Dowager's roar. I'm now at the airlock. Comet tails! She doesn't answer. I'm turning on the visual monitor—she's on the floor. Looks as if she's unconscious."

There was the sound of banging and Fargo swearing. "I can't open the airlock! She must have double-locked it from the inside."

74

"Fargo!" Norby yelled. "The door will open if you give the computer emergency code five-two!"

"Thanks, Norby. I forgot. Punching it in. There—the door's open now, and I'm dragging the Dowager into the ship. She's breathing okay, but she's out cold."

"But what happened to her?" Jeff asked. "Do you still have a headache?"

"Yes, and it's getting worse. Maybe it's the vibrations from the cloud. Perhaps the Dowager began to get a headache and was angry or upset—evidently she breathed out flame because there's a big smudge on the inside of the airlock's outer door."

"Fargo!" Norby shouted. "Shut the inner door of the airlock! I'm picking up data relayed to the Jamyn computer, and according to the ship's monitors, alien material is entering the lock from outside."

Jeff could hear the clear sound of the inner door slamming shut and then his brother said, "No use, although I can't understand how the stuff is creeping in around the airlock seals. It's almost invisible at first, but once beyond the seal it coalesces into tendrils of thick yellowish gas, or whatever it is."

"Put on a space suit," Jeff said. "Protect yourself."

"If it bypasses the ship's airlock, it will penetrate a space suit. I'm going to the control room and get us out of here as quickly as possible."

In another moment his voice, considerably subdued, came back. "Sorry, folks. The ship won't respond. I can see a film of yellowish something over the computer controls. The antigrav hover seems to be functioning perfectly so we won't crash onto Jamya, but we can't get back."

"If the cloud knocked out the Dowager Dragon and headed straight for the computer controls, it must be intelligent," Norby said. "Don't let it touch you, Fargo."

Fargo laughed. "As if I had any control over this pirate of a cloud that's taken my ship. What do you suggest I do, serenade it?"

"Is the Dowager awake? Perhaps she can talk to it," said Mentor First.

"According to the visual monitor she's still unconscious. Besides, how do you talk to a cloud?"

"It's in the computer, so maybe it will talk to you, or at least listen to what you say," Jeff said.

"I'm glad somebody in the Wells family has brains." Fargo said, "Hello there, alien cloud, this is your local human, Fargo Wells speaking. I'd appreciate it if we set up a person-to-person dialogue . . ."

"What happened?" Albany shouted.

"Not a thing. I touched one of the computer switches just for fun but it's dead. I shall persevere with this one-way conversation, especially since my headache is going away. Perhaps the cloud radiates energy only when it's hungry and now it's full from eating the ship's energy. You know, this could be an interesting adventure . . ."

"Is life support still operating?" Albany said.

"I'm still breathing, love. Panting a bit with loneliness for you, but alive and well. The ship's air is still circulating and the lights are on also. I guess I'm in no danger, but I wish the cloud *were* intelligent so I could talk to it. Right now it's like a large furry animal that's sniffing around and may very well leave as soon as it finds out we're not its kind."

"I've tried to make the main computer here give instructions to the ship's computer, but it won't work," Norby said. "That small amount of cloud that's inside the ship either has a great deal of power or it's still connected to the power of the rest of the cloud."

"I am going to take my ship to rescue you," Mentor First said. "We will lock airlocks—"

"No!" Fargo yelled. "If you come here the cloud will enter your airlock and probably you, just as it's taken over this computer. Stay where you are!"

"I'll come up alone and get you," Norby said.

"You can't rescue me, or the Dowager, without turning off your field, and then you'll be vulnerable, Norby. I insist that everyone stay safely on the surface of Jamya while we wait for this foggy critter to stoke up and move on. Except that it seems to be moving in—there's a big ropy tendril of fog . . ."

Silence. And Norby finally said, "All contact with the *Hopeful* has been broken off."

9

Disappearance

"I am going to my ship," Mentor First said. "Whatever the risk, I must go to Fargo's aid."

"I'm going with you," Albany said. Her face was pale but her voice was resolute.

"Don't be idiots!" Norby waved his arms and extended his half a head up as far as it would go. "That's the only ship on the planet now that the *Hopeful* is unavailable and you should save it for the last emergency. In the meantime . . ."

Jeff took Norby's hand.—Don't tell them. Don't ask if it's okay, because Albany and Mentor First will say it isn't. Let's leave, Norby.

Norby yanked Jeff off his feet so quickly that his stomach lurched, but fortunately the banquet stayed down as the boy and robot soared up to the cloud layer threatening Jamya.

—My protective field is on, Jeff. It's our only protection against whatever danger's up there.

You'll have to hold on to me and stay in it the whole time.

—All right, Norby. I'll try. There's the *Hopeful*, and the airlock is now completely open!

Jeff didn't stop to think about the fact that he could see the ship through what had been a thick cloud until he realized that Norby was zooming through a strange tunnel of clear space, with the ship at the other end.

Norby flew right into the airlock, dragging Jeff with him, and stopped abruptly at the sight of the Dowager Dragon lying on the floor of the ship.

—The ship's maintaining its position on antigrav, and the inside artificial gravity is on, so the computer hasn't gone completely haywire even if it won't respond to communications. Shall I plug into it here?

—No, Norby. Check the air. With the airlock open, the air in the ship should be not only very thin this high up but also contaminated by the cloud. The Dowager is still breathing but it may be killing her.

Norby's sensor wire went out and Jeff waited, still holding onto Norby's hand, until he heard the next telepathic message.

—Breathable air, Jeff. Thinner than normal, but not as thin as it ought to be.

—Contamination?

—A little. If you get outside my protective field, you might sneeze some, but it won't kill you.

—Then let go, Norby. I know we said I'd stay inside your field for protection, but the Dowager and Fargo can't, so I might as well experiment.

Besides, I'll soon use up the oxygen enclosed by your field.

Norby dropped Jeff's hand and turned off his protective field. Instantly, Jeff sneezed, for the air smelt like a chem lab without proper ventilation. His eyes began to water.

"Fargo!" Jeff yelled.

"That's odd," Norby said. "After you sneezed, the air started to clear up. There's a steady stream of the irritating particles going out the airlock."

"We have to find Fargo." Jeff ran to the control room. It was empty.

Norby plugged himself into the computer and shut all his eyes, but after only a moment he opened them and said, "This computer's data banks have been wiped clean. Except for an unconscious dragon, there's nobody home in this ship."

"I can't believe that. Help me search." He and Norby went to the cabin, but it was empty too. Jeff searched every cranny in the ship where a human being might fit, but Fargo was just not anywhere.

"He's missing, Jeff. But where did he go—we didn't see him in the tunnel, and besides, without antigrav, he'd have fallen through the fog."

"Don't say that. Perhaps he did fall—wait—maybe he took off the Dowager's antigrav collar . . ." Jeff and Norby went back to her. She was still wearing her collar.

"The Dowager breathed fire at something she thought was coming to kill her—look at that burn mark inside the lock—and after she fell, Fargo opened the inner door and dragged her inside the ship," Norby said. "She's been unconscious ever since, so only Fargo could have opened the outer door."

"My brother wouldn't do anything so stupid, in a space ship hovering on antigrav almost at the top of a planet's atmosphere, with an alien cloud outside. Fargo's intelligent and efficient in spite of his love of danger . . ." Jeff stopped, appalled.

"That's just it, Jeff. Fargo likes derring-do. If the cloud sent a tendril of fog into the control room the way Fargo said it did, then he might very well have followed it."

"He said it took over the computer—that must be when the data banks were wiped out—and then when he tried to touch the fog it left the computer because it's not there now. In fact, there aren't any specific tendrils of fog here . . ."

"You spoke too soon, Jeff."

A ghostly finger of fog snaked through the open airlock and into the ship, hugging the wall across from Jeff. It didn't have eyes, but Jeff had the eerie feeling that it was examining him.

"Norby! Protect yourself! Put on your field so the fog won't do to you what it did to the computer."

"Okay, Jeff, but I think you ought to hold onto me and I'll protect you, too."

"The dragon's moving—maybe she needs protection first."

The Dowager groaned and sat up, her eyelids fluttering open. "How did you get here, Jeff Wells? Where is your brother Fargo?"

"Norby brought me to the ship. I don't know where Fargo is. What did the fog do to you?"

"When it started to creep into the airlock, molecule by molecule I suppose, I flamed at it. Some of it seemed to dissolve, but it kept coming, wrapping me up the way we do our newborn dragons. Finally I couldn't breathe and blacked out."

"Did you sense anything in particular? I mean . . ." Jeff didn't want to make his question too specific, for the groggy dragon might read into her sense memories what Jeff was hinting at. " . . .did you react to the fog as if, I mean . . ."

"I sensed curiosity, young human. Intense curiosity. That means the fog is an entity of some sort, and moreover it is a creature of intelligence."

Jeff nodded. "Norby and I just flew up through a weird tunnel in the fog. I did not sense any intelligence, but if it made the tunnel for us . . ."

"Precisely, young Jeff. You must be afraid that because the fog enclosed me and rendered me unconscious, it may have changed me in some way."

"Yes, ma'am. Do you think it did?"

The dragon blinked. "Not that I can tell. I seem to be in full possession of all my ordinary faculties plus my usual list of ailments. The only thing added, besides weakness, is the shame of not having helped at all. I came up here to try to communicate with this unusual entity, but instead I flamed at it as if I were one of my primitive dragon ancestors, ready to fight anything that seems dangerous. But it must be truly dangerous if your handsome brother is missing."

"He must be outside the ship, ma'am, but I don't see how."

While the Dowager talked, Norby had left for the control room again, and now he returned. "I think that if Fargo had planned to leave the ship he'd have tried to leave a note, knowing that ship to planet communications were out, but I haven't been able to find one. Of course, if he left one in the computer, it's been deleted."

Jeff, Norby, and the dragon stared at each other.

Jeff finally managed to say what he was thinking. "Fargo can't possibly have survived if he stepped outside."

"I will go and see," the Dowager said, stretching her scaly legs and shaking her wings. "Perhaps the tunnel is not as smooth as it looks, and Fargo is concealed behind a bulge in the cloud somewhere."

"It's not safe," Jeff said.

"My dear young human, I do not plan to step off the airlock rim into that unpleasant chemical mixture out there. I will fly through the tunnel. I think I can still manage."

Without waiting for Jeff's approval, the Dowager walked into the airlock. She paused, looking at the invading arm of fog only a couple of centimeters from her large body.

"The stuff looks thicker now, more like whipped kafoogle juice. I never liked kafoogle juice." She reached toward the tendril with her right foreclaw.

"Don't touch it!" Jeff yelled. "Fargo said something about a big ropy tendril of fog coming into the control room. Then all communications were lost."

"Maybe the fog dissolves organic beings," Norby said. "Better not touch it, Your Dragonness, and try not to touch the sides of the tunnel with your wings."

"Please don't, ma'am," Jeff said, struggling to keep from crying, for he had realized that Norby could be right. Fargo would have come back, or shouted out, if he'd gone out into the fog without falling through or—Jeff shuddered—being dissolved.

"Bah! I was a Grand Dragon and the daughter of a Grand Dragon. I'm not afraid of smelly soup that thinks it can outsmart the dragons of Jamya!" She poked at the tendril, which did indeed look much thicker.

Nothing happened. The dragon peered at her own claw. "It certainly hasn't dissolved this part of my body." Where upon she drew back her right hind leg and bestowed a mighty kick on the tendril.

"Oof!" The Dowager picked herself up from the airlock floor, for the kick had bounced off the tendril and she hadn't been prepared for that.

"Like hitting something rubber," Jeff said. "Ma'am, if the stuff is that thick, I'll be able to go out without wings."

"Let me explore first, Jeff," the Dowager said. "I don't trust any of it." She teetered on the rim of the airlock, spread her wings and flew into the tunnel.

"Norby, the tunnel's not heading down to the planet any more! The Dowager's heading up, out of the atmosphere! She won't be able to breathe at the end of the tunnel!"

Norby hurled himself out of the airlock, ignoring Jeff's outstretched hand. Alone, the little robot propelled his barrel body through the tunnel with Jeff shouting "Take me with you!" until Norby disappeared up the curve.

Jeff put one foot out of the airlock, testing the thick cloud surface of the tunnel floor. His foot sank into the stuff and he was sure that his whole body would fall through, but suddenly the fog seemed to congeal and he quickly withdrew. When he tested the surface again, his foot bounced back. The tunnel floor had solidified.

Just before Jeff could step out with both feet, Norby zoomed down the tunnel with the large dragon in tow within his protective field. Jeff sprang back into the ship, for there wasn't room for him when the Dowager was inside the airlock.

As Norby released her she sputtered, "It tricked us! I shot out of the tunnel into *space*! I'd have died if Norby hadn't come, for the tunnel was starting to close behind me."

"Then how did you get through, Norby?"

"I condensed my protective field to a harder energy shell around me and just—please excuse the expression—barreled through. When I expanded my field to include Her Dragonness, the fog made way for us."

"Perhaps it knows royalty when it encounters it," said the Dowager, clumping into the ship and sitting down on her haunches in front of the airlock. "I'm afraid I didn't see Fargo anywhere."

"Not exactly," Norby said.

"What do you mean?" Jeff started to grab Norby to shake him but his hands slid off the field barrier. Norby, who talked through his hat anyway because he had no mouth, was now talking through his sensor wire, sticking a millimeter out of the field.

"I may have been mistaken—of course, I'm hardly ever mistaken, since the perfection of my parts—"

"Norby!"

Norby's metal eyelids shut half way, his arms drooped, and he managed to look upset. "On the way back, my rear eyes caught a glimpse of something. Something like a face."

"A face?"

"A huge face. The tunnel closed in behind me and for a moment the thick wall looked an awful lot like Fargo."

10

Monos

"That's impossible," Jeff said, hoping to reassure himself if he said the words out loud. It didn't work. "Unless—if Fargo's out there, perhaps a reflection—no, he couldn't be out there. He'd fall through."

"Of course it's impossible." The Dowager's bulk blocked Jeff's view out the airlock. "I saw no such reflection. Without wings or antigrav your brother couldn't survive."

"I'm trying to remember whether or not he has one of the dragons' antigrav collars," Jeff said, desperately searching for an explanation.

"Then he would have hailed us," the Dowager said, stroking her broken fang. "There could not have been a reflection of Fargo's face. Your robot must be malfunctioning."

"I never! Well, hardly ever, and furthermore . . ." Norby stopped abruptly and rose on antigrav until he was as high as the dragon.

"Your Dragonness, would you be so kind as to move out of the way so I can check my sensor readings? I am getting something strange . . ."

"I think we should shut the airlock and rest until we decide what to do about this situation," the dragon said, moving only slightly aside. She yawned and rubbed her eyes. "I am tired. I am not accustomed to flying at this age."

Now Norby was blocking Jeff's view, hanging in the open door of the airlock, his back eyes shut.

"See anything, Norby?" Jeff asked.

"The fog next to the ship seems to be clearing up and—Jeff, I'm sorry. I think I *am* malfunctioning."

Jeff rushed to Norby, pulling him down until it was possible to see over the robot's hat. The tunnel had gone, yet the cloud did seem thinner directly in front of the airlock, with thin strands of mist whirling by, obscuring the view.

"What is it, Norby? What did you sense?"

"I can't trust my sensors any more. I thought the cloud was congealing out there."

"Into another tunnel?"

"No, Jeff. Into—that."

Jeff looked out again. There were no solidifying arms of cloud reaching into the ship. Instead, the cloud layer before the airlock had flattened and broadened, leaving a clear space above it. As Jeff watched, the boundaries of the flat space congealed, and the cloud layer forming the bottom of the space began to look different.

"What's going on!" the dragon shouted, peering over both Jeff and Norby. "Is that grass out there?"

"Sure looks like it," Norby said. "I'd say that a rose garden is beginning to shape up toward the back, too."

The space in the cloud was now a place, and a place that seemed oddly familiar to Jeff.

"I know this scene," Jeff said slowly. "I've been here."

"Think, Jeff," Norby said. "Where?"

"On Earth. Maine, I think. I was just a kid. Look—now there's a white stone bird bath in the rose garden. And a bench in front of the garden, on the lawn. I think those trees beyond the back hedge are pine trees."

"What place are you talking about?" the dragon asked.

"This looks like the back yard of my grand-uncle's summer house. Our family used to visit there when I was a child, before my parents were killed. Fargo loved that back yard, for he'd been going there long before I was born."

Starting at the airlock's outer door, a semicircle of green lawn stretched out to the white slatted bench in front of the rose garden that was now in full bloom, as if it were the best of Maine summers. Faint mist swirled in front of the flowers so their colors were muted, and there were no bees or butterflies hovering over the blooms.

"Anything missing, Jeff?" Norby asked.

"The jungle gym and swings, but I think they were added after I was born."

"A pretty place," said the dragon, standing behind them.

"Hello, Jeff."

"Fargo!"

He was just visible in the mist between the trees. "How do you like this place?" he said, walking up to the hedge and opening a green gate Jeff hadn't noticed there. He came on through a little path in the rose garden.

"I always wanted a gate in the hedge and a path in the garden, remember, Jeff?"

"Yes, Fargo. Are you all right?"

"Fine. Never better. Come out on the lawn—it will hold us. The place is real."

"Humph!" The dragon snorted. "Impossible."

"Maybe not," Jeff said, stepping out of the lock onto what felt like mushy but reasonably solid ground.

"I'm coming out with you, Jeff. There's something not quite right..." Norby was extending his sensor wire out of his protective field so he could scan the area when a thick arm of fog shot out between two pine trees, aimed at Norby.

"Norby!" Jeff shouted. "Protect yourself!"

The arm wound around Norby but Jeff could see a clear space, only a few centimeters wide, separating the robot's body from the fog. Norby drew in his sensor wire to make the field tighter and the eerie arm spread out to form a giant fist enveloping him.

Then the fist threw Norby into the ship, pushed back the dragon, and slammed the airlock shut. Jeff could not reenter the ship without passing through a section of cloud that now resembled an iron fence.

"It knows I want to talk to you alone, Jeff."

Jeff was more angry than frightened. "And just what is this 'it' that's now a friend of yours?"

"Come, sit down on the garden bench and I'll explain everything."

"I want Norby. Tell your 'it' to open the airlock and let him out."

"Please, Jeff. You will not be harmed."

Reluctantly, Jeff sat down on the white bench. "Where were you when Norby and the dragon searched?"

"This cloud is huge, Jeff. It encircles the planet. Lots of room. I think the cloud should have a name. Any ideas?"

"You've probably already thought of one. When I was small and you'd tell me stories, you were always good at thinking up interesting names."

"I want you to name the cloud. Please."

Jeff shivered. The air was not exactly cold but there was no warmth, and the light on the garden was too pale, without the richness of sunlight on Earth. "Fargo, what's wrong? Why didn't you radio that you were going to leave the ship? And why did you?"

"Communications with Jamya stopped working. And since I couldn't talk to you people, and the dragon was still out cold, I thought I'd take a walk. The place looked solid."

"But it wasn't solid when Norby and the Dowager flew out to look for you. Where did you go? Why didn't you let Norby know you were out in the fog? We've been so worried."

"I am sorry. I was—busy."

"But are you sure you're all right?" Jeff reached out to touch him but didn't succeed because Fargo stood up and walked over to the biggest bush in the rose garden.

"Remember these, Jeff? So dark red they're almost black."

Jeff walked up to the rose bush and plucked the largest, darkest rose. The flower seemed curiously light in weight, and as he tried to touch the petals with his other hand, the whole thing dissolved into a mist that slid away from him. Fargo walked away from Jeff, back to the bench.

"Fargo, I'm coming over to pick you up. I'm as tall as you are now and we weigh about the same—or do we? If I pick you up off the grass will you dissolve, too?"

It was Fargo's face but Jeff saw that the blue eyes were missing the expressiveness so characteristic of his brother. No mischievous twinkle; no dark sadness. Nothing but form—without real substance.

"All I want is to talk with you for a while, Jeff. Please don't question—"

"You said all this was real, but it isn't. You lied."

"Everything in the universe is real, Jeff. You and I are part of the universe, aren't we? Are we not real?"

"No, you aren't. If you think you're real, I dare you to come with me into the ship without leaving an umbilical cord of fog attaching yourself to—"

"That's enough! All I asked was that you give a name to the cloud that is even now creating this space and this breathable atmosphere for our conversation. The cloud is sustaining your life and mine and all it asks is that it be given a name. Is that too much to ask?"

"It's *you* who asks for a name. You aren't Fargo. You are the immense entity that destroyed my brother and is destroying the entire planet of Jamya!"

"You make many assumptions. Give me a name and I will give you back your brother."

"Ah—you are the cloud, then? The cloud, referring to itself as 'I'?"

The image of Fargo bowed its head. "Yes. I need a name."

Jeff thought. "Are you one entity, or many that join?"

"I am one. I am only myself. There is no other."

"Okay. Then I name you 'Monos.' "

The image of Fargo pressed its hands together. "Excellent. I thank you."

"Now give me back my brother!"

11

Brothers?

The false image of Fargo seemed to quiver from the force of Jeff's words. The image made no sound, but gradually it blurred, crumpling into a horrible misshapen blob that slowly slid back into the grass and disappeared.

"Fargo! Where are you! Monos, you blasted alien, you promised to give him back!"

The garden was still, each rose less distinct than before. Jeff tried to push aside the make-believe fence in front of the *Hopeful's* airlock but it wouldn't budge. He could not go back into the ship.

"Norby!" There was no answer. Jeff had never felt so alone in his life. He wanted Norby worse than he ever had, but he knew it was selfish to call for Norby's help when the alien cloud might be much more dangerous to robots than to humans. He remembered the blank data banks of the ship's computer and did not call for Norby again.

Could Monos be somehow watching and judging him, condemning him for being a frightened child instead of a brave adult human? Jeff stifled a sob and realized that more than anything else he wanted his brother back.

"Hi ya, Jeff! Stop looking so worried about me, little brother. Here I am, safe and sound."

This Fargo looked much more solid, and he smiled just the way Fargo always did when he was happy about being in an exciting situation. When Fargo leapt over the white gate in the hedge, that settled it for Jeff. This Fargo was not attached to the false ground that was the cloud.

Jeff ran to him and they put their arms around each other.

"You feel real."

"I'm as real as real can be, Jeff. Missing a couple of hours of consciousness, but otherwise intact. This alien whosis is very big and not very bright, you know."

"I didn't. Can you communicate with the cloud?"

"I can try."

"Tell it to let me open the airlock. I want to make sure Norby's okay. Tell it not to harm Norby in any way."

"The cloud read my mind—that's how it made that silly image of me—so it knows that it must not harm the robot you love. Or anything you love, even the oldest dragon. She's still inside, isn't she?"

"Yes, and probably hopping mad by now—hey! The fence has gone and the airlock's open! Can Monos hear us?"

"I'm sure it can. Hi, Norby. You'd better scan me to assure Jeff that I'm real. I think that's one of the reasons Jeff wanted to see you."

Norby stood at the outer door of the lock, staring at Fargo. His sensor wire was out, and beyond him the Dowager Dragon was glaring at both humans.

"I have been insulted, attacked . . ." the dragon began, each word accompanied by a puff of smoke.

"On the contrary, madam, it was you who attacked the entity which my brother has named Monos. Although the entity is large, it does not appreciate even a small portion of its anatomy being vaporized."

Trying not to show any expression in his face, Jeff walked up to Norby and touched him. The protective field was off.

—Norby, the cloud made an illusion of Fargo before. I must know if this is the organic Fargo.

—Down to the last DNA helix in every cell, Jeff.

Jeff turned. "Norby says you're real, Fargo. Forgive me, but I had to check."

"Sure, little brother. I understand. I'd have done the same." Fargo bowed to the Dowager, who had shoved Norby aside and was plowing over the phony grass toward him. "We meet again, Your Dragonness."

"You can tell your friend the so-called cloud that it must go away and leave Jamya before the planet dies."

When Fargo just shrugged, Jeff quickly said, "We have no special language to communicate with the cloud, ma'am. I believe it hears us whenever we speak."

"Well, when are you going to go away, Monos?"

Nobody said anything, until finally Fargo shrugged again. "I suppose it's still learning about us. Look—there's the sort of appendage that grabbed me when I opened the airlock."

A many-fingered hand had arisen from the rose garden, one finger pointed at the airlock. As Jeff watched, his skin crawling, the hand seemed to float through the garden into the grass, past the two humans and the dragon. It stopped just at the open airlock.

Norby said, "I'm putting up my field again." And just in time, for the hand covered Norby's barrel, sliding over the invisible field that showed up as a space in the cloud. This time the cloud hand didn't throw Norby but gently picked him up and deposited him in Jeff's arms.

The slippery field-covered robot rested in Jeff's arms until the hand withdrew, and suddenly Jeff could feel Norby's metal cold against his skin.

—I think it's safe, Jeff. I caught a whiff of thought from that blasted creature. I detected no intent to harm me.

—But something's very wrong, and I don't know what.

The ghostly hand beckoned.

"Who is it ordering around, I'd like to know," said the dragon, rustling her wings. "This farcical business has gone on long enough. Shall I flame Monos at its phony wrist?"

"No," Jeff said. "Let's follow it into the ship. That must be where it wants us to go."

Jeff carried Norby and the dragon clumped along behind into the airlock. The hand shrank down to a small knob at the end of a long string, but it followed the dragon and Jeff.

"Come on, Fargo!" Jeff yelled, noticing that his brother was still standing out on the fake grass.

"Is it safe? Shouldn't one of us stay out here as long as Monos has put part of itself into the ship?"

The knob immediately swelled to become a hand and, like a cobra ready to strike, reared up and beckoned to Fargo.

"I think you'd better come inside," Jeff said. "Monos knows that even if we shut the airlock, molecules of itself can enter the ship and maintain contact with the hand."

Fargo walked inside the ship. "All the same, we'd better not shut the door."

Jeff touched Fargo's arm to make telepathic contact.

—We'll shut the door and then put on suits and flood the ship with sleep gas. It might not work but then it might. We'd be rid of the cloud at least inside the ship.

Norby, hearing the telepathic words because he was still in Jeff's arms, floated out on antigrav, closed the door, and handed the Wells brothers their space suits.

"Sorry, Your Dragonness, but you'll have to take another nap. Better get comfortable. We don't have a suit big enough for you," Norby said.

"Look!" Jeff pointed to the string of fog that had come in with them. "It's dissolving even before we turn on the gas!"

"No!" Fargo yelled. "Don't do this! It's dangerous!"

At that moment there was a horrifying clash of metal against metal and for a few seconds the ship and everybody in it vibrated. Fargo sat down on the floor with his head in his hands, moaning.

The airlock opened and Albany Jones ran through. "Mentor First managed to get his ship through the fog to find you, and we've connected airlocks."

There was a peculiar smell and then Mentor First, stooping to fit in the *Hopeful*'s airlock, came through. "I've sprayed both airlocks with a special sealant we use on Jamya. I don't think the cloud will be able to enter either ship now."

"Darling!" Albany was bending over Fargo. "Are you ill?"

"Just a queasy sensation, when I smelled the spray. Perhaps I'm allergic to that sealant."

"He was the prisoner of the cloud for a while," Jeff said, his own thoughts frightening him. "The cloud has unusual abilities to make illusory objects from what it reads in our minds. It read Fargo's mind and made a garden we had as children. It also made an illusion of Fargo that for a moment fooled me. But the illusion would have dissolved inside the ship, cut off from the rest of the cloud."

"Just like the hand that came in with us," the dragon said. "I am almost sorry that it's gone, for I never had a chance to try my communicative abilities on it. Perhaps I never had any. I certainly didn't make any use of them this time, when Jamya is in such danger."

"It's cold and dark all over the planet, and the dragons are very afraid," Albany said. "Fargo, are you sure you're all right?" As she helped him to his feet Jeff saw that Fargo was terribly pale, his black hair plastered onto his sweaty forehead and his dark blue eyes wide, the pupils dilated.

"Albany, I love you. No matter what, I love you."

She put her arms around him. "Come on, chum, you've had a nasty experience but you're going to be okay now. I love you, too." She kissed him, at length.

"Ah," said the dragon. "It must be interesting to have two sexes. Too bad I'm too old to study the phenomenon."

—Norby, is Fargo damaged in some way?

—No, Jeff. I get the same readings I always did for his cellular and organ structure.

—But what about his brain patterns?

—I'll check . . .

Albany pushed Fargo away. "You're not Fargo! Who are you?"

12

WHAT IS DEATH?

"I am Fargo."

Norby stepped toward him. "You're the body of Fargo Wells but you have different brain patterns."

"I know all that Fargo knows."

"You're part of Monos, aren't you?" Jeff asked, his voice hoarse. The real Fargo must be dead.

"I—I must be Fargo . . ." The beloved face of Jeff's brother, so familiar and yet now so strange, contorted as if he was in agony. "It is cruel of you to say that I am not Fargo. I don't like any of you—"

Albany slapped his face. "Where is Fargo? *My* Fargo? Have you taken over his body? If so, get out of it!"

"I cannot. I am bound . . . trapped . . ."

"Scan the body again, Norby," Jeff said. "Find out if the cloud we're calling Monos has inserted itself into Fargo's brain so it can control him."

"You don't understand," Norby said. "There isn't any alien matter in Fargo's brain, or anywhere in his body. This person is the biological Fargo. This person, however, has brain patterns that are completely different, patterns that are not superimposed on Fargo's."

"You mean Fargo's mind has been destroyed?" Albany took out her gun. "You monster!"

"I have always been this way," the replica of Fargo said. "This biological individual has never been different."

Albany pointed the gun at the replica. "I'll stun it, and then we'll do a more careful scanning of the brain, perhaps find Fargo—"

"No," Jeff said. "I think it means what it says. This is a replica of Fargo that has never had Fargo's brain patterns, only those generated by Monos. Am I correct?"

"You are correct." The replica was still sweating, pale and obviously frightened. "I must go outside at once."

"If you try it I'll stun you," Albany said. "You can't go anywhere until you tell us where Fargo is."

"The biological individual you knew does not exist," said the replica, sagging against the wall. "I must leave."

"Why?" asked the dragon, touching his hair with one claw.

He looked up at her. "I wanted to experience—your experience. Your—individuality. All of you—robot, human, or Jamyn—all of you are separate from each other. Individual. I do not understand this. I wanted to know."

"But why do you want to leave the ship so desperately?"

Tears began to stream from the replica's eyes. "I am not sure. I feel lost, apart, frightened. Am I dying?"

"No," Norby said. "Your body scan still shows that you are physically healthy, even if you're very disturbed."

"All organic beings die," Mentor First said in his deep voice. "In fact, everything dies, even robots. Even sentient clouds of alien matter, like you, for Monos will die when the universe does."

When the replica began to sob, the dragon held him close to her scaly chest.

"Death isn't so terrible," she said. "I'm going to die soon and I don't mind."

"I mind!" The cry was of anguish. "What is death?"

"An ending. You wouldn't want to read a story that didn't have an end, would you?" the dragon asked.

"I do not understand about endings. I have always existed but now I am separate from myself. I am having thoughts, experiences that Monos will never know!"

"When did Monos come to this solar system?" Jeff asked.

"Long ago. The third planet was cool and suitable. I—Monos—rested. There was no sense of time, no real memory. No identity. I was not aware of—myself. Not conscious."

"Until when?" Jeff asked, knowing the answer.

"In your terminology it would be called 'today.' I

received messages, strange things that stirred my mind, awakened me to myself, to the universe. I came to find out."

"My fault," Norby said, withdrawing his head until only the tops of his eyes showed. "I shouldn't have made the holov transmission so strong."

"Monos," the Dowager Dragon said in an amused tone, "I don't blame you for being confused after being awakened to consciousness by the holov broadcast of my daughter's birthday party. With that, and eating our force field, it's a wonder you don't have severe mental indigestion!"

"Perhaps that is what I have experienced," the replica said sadly. "All I know now is that I feel as if I am about to die inside this ship. I must go outside and return to Monos. Please, you creatures and robots, have pity on me."

"Why should we pity you?" Albany said grimly. "You had no pity on Fargo when you destroyed his individuality."

"I didn't think the individual mind mattered, not when he could become part of me—I mean of Monos." A fleeting, almost Fargo-like smile touched the tortured face. "The limitations of life on this level, this separate individuality of mortal creatures! Yet you live with such intensity! I have a strange desire to stay with you, on this level, but I know that is not possible. My mind will die if I don't go back. Please, Jeff, come with me—only you. I do not believe that Monos trusts the other organics, and the robots would be endangered. Separate your ships so the garden can be recreated."

"Norby," Jeff said, "you and Mentor First must

go in his ship. Put the ship's shields up and wait until this is over."

"I want to go with you, Jeff!"

"No, Norby. I just want to ask Monos a few questions."

Albany was holding tightly to her gun. "I'm going along to protect you, Jeff."

The dragon chuckled. "My dear human female, you and I have much in common. Under emotional stress we revert to the primitive female trait of protecting others with claw and fang. I think that you and I will just watch."

The replica smiled wanly. "From Fargo's memories I can repeat the expression, 'The female of the species is more deadly than the male.' Put away the gun, Albany. It could kill me but it's of no use against Monos. Please, Jeff, go outside with me."

Norby argued some more, but when Jeff insisted, Mentor First scooped up his robot son, strode through the airlocks and then the ships separated. Jeff looked out and saw the garden shimmer into a semblance of reality. He nodded to the replica.

"We can go outside, now. Will you be all right there?"

"I think so." With eyes that were exact physical replicas of Fargo's, the replica gazed out into Monos. "Strange. I don't know why, but I am afraid."

The dragon touched Jeff.—The replica doesn't realize that it can't live with us and it can't live with Monos.

—I know, ma'am. I'm afraid, too.

—Then you stay here with Albany. I will go with

the replica. My life doesn't matter.

—No, Your Dragonness. Even this Fargo is my brother.

Gently, Jeff detached the dragon's grip from his arm and took the replica by the hand. "Come on outside."

Together, they walked through the open airlock onto the grass that seemed less defined than before. Albany waited in the airlock, the dragon standing behind her.

"Jeff," Albany said, "tell Monos I will know if it tries to substitute another replica for Fargo."

"It hears you, Albany. I hope." Jeff turned to the replica. "Does it hear all of us, or only you, now?"

"I do not know! Monos! I cannot sense your thoughts! Can you hear me? Will our minds be one again?" The replica's eyes were wild with horror. "I am still separate! Lost!"

"You're just an individual, sir. Like the rest of us."

"I want to die! Monos! Eat my body so I may be part of you again, my brain patterns those of Monos—"

Jeff grabbed the replica. "Can Monos make the real Fargo, with the right brain patterns?"

"I don't know. Since this body was made I—this individual before you—have been thinking like a human because I must. I can no longer tell you what Monos can do."

Jeff looked up at the mistiness hanging over the illusion of a garden. "Monos! If you hear us, please—"

Suddenly two arms of solidified fog shot up from

the grass and embraced Jeff, holding him tightly. "What's this for!"

"I think that Monos is going to try again," the replica said. "Perhaps it sensed one of my thoughts—that it should try superimposing itself upon a living individual, keeping that individual connected to itself. I am no longer connected and perhaps cannot join again. Before you take Jeff, Monos, join me to you again, even if I have to die."

Jeff could not move. He saw that the false iron fence again blocked exit from the ship, so that Albany and the dragon were trapped inside. He wondered if Norby and Mentor First were watching from the other ship, if its scanners worked.

Another snakelike extension of fog wound itself around the replica, the coils tightening rapidly.

"Is death painful, young Jeff?"

"I don't know. Maybe if you just let go . . ."

The replica smiled as the coil wrapped around his neck. "I have enjoyed my memories—*his* memories of you, Jeff. Of being brothers. Of playing in this garden, and watching my—his— little brother play in it. Goodbye."

The coils squeezed, but the light had already left the replica's eyes.

13

CONVERSATION

Only the replica has died, Jeff told himself. Not my real brother. Only a biological replica with mind patterns from Monos, not Fargo—and yet . . .

Jeff watched the replica's body sag in death, the face gray. Fargo's face.

"Goodbye," Jeff whispered. "I'm so sorry. You were alive, and biologically as human as Fargo. You didn't deserve to die, either."

To Jeff's astonishment, tentacles bearing oddly human hands sprouted from the thick coil of cloud around the dead replica. These hands felt all over the body, pressing and probing as if not sure that the replica was actually dead.

Forgetting that Monos now had no mouth with which to answer him, Jeff yelled, "You didn't try to take him back! You killed the replica just the way you killed my brother. You are a monster!"

One of the pine trees on the other side of the garden hedge quivered, its form changing to an immense, nebulous imitation of a human mouth. The grotesque apparition opened and a voice like a dying sigh spoke to Jeff.

"That part of me which entered your ship became separate, and I did not know what to do. When it came back outside the ship with you it was a stranger. It called to me, asking to be taken back into me. I was deciding what to do. I would have taken it. I do not understand what happened."

Trying to get away, Jeff struggled against the imitation arms keeping him helpless. They were too strong, and the pressure on his body only increased. He tried to relax so he could keep breathing.

"Why did that separate part of me become so different, so quickly?" the mouth of Monos asked. "I do not die—why should it have died?"

"You killed him!"

"That is not true. I did not know it was dead until I examined the body just now. How could this have happened?"

"You know he wanted to become part of you again, but you hesitated. Why?"

"I told you. The replica was not myself and I had to decide. Why did it not wish to stay with you?"

"His mind wasn't human, so living with us would have been very difficult. He wanted to return to you, to become part of you once more. You tell *me* what happened, Monos. Did you somehow tell the replica to kill himself?"

"No. I do not understand the replica's death, but I must accept what has happened." The false hands of Monos dragged the replica's body to the ground where it began to break up. Although there was no bleeding because the body was already dead, the sight was so gruesome that Jeff had to shut his eyes.

Shuddering, he said, "You're eating the replica, just the way you ate my brother."

"This is the only way I can take the replica back into myself. Furthermore, I must reuse the material. If that is eating, then it is necessary."

Jeff opened his eyes and saw that the replica's body had already vanished into the ground. The mouth of Monos now had a huge, vaguely human eye above it, staring at Jeff.

"I see the expression on your face, human. You hate me."

"Yes. You may not have killed the replica on purpose but you did deliberately kill my brother. You are a murderer."

"I know about the concept of murder. Information about murder was in your computer, and in your brother's brain. I destroyed only his organic body but all the information in his brain is now part of me. Therefore your brother still exists and I did not commit murder."

"You *are* a murderer! Fargo was a separate being, part of nothing else. You destroyed the aspect of Fargo that made him different from all other beings—his personality."

"I do not understand. How can that brother of yours be dead when he is part of me?"

Despairing of ever making such a creature understand, Jeff twisted his head, hoping that Albany or the dragon would help him convince Monos of his crime. To his horror he saw that the fake iron fence had become a steel slab enclosing the entire garden and, as he watched, it extended behind the pine trees. Both ships were beyond the barrier and Jeff was completely alone with Monos.

There was one molecule of hope left to Jeff. The arms holding him had not pressed too tightly yet. Monos was not at the moment trying to kill him. Monos wanted to talk. Very well, thought Jeff. We'll have conversation.

"Monos, you possess all the memories Fargo's brain contained when you assimilated him. What you don't understand is that the facts stored in brain proteins are not the same thing as the living brain patterns that make a person who he is. If you eat an individual and incorporate his stored memories he still dies as an individual no matter how much knowledge you gain—unless you permit his brain patterns to take over yours, or at least share—"

"I must be myself!" The mouth that had been the facsimile of a tree quivered—with fear? Rage? As Jeff wondered what the retribution would be, the mouth solidified with a firm, cruel tightness to the lips. The eye above it seemed to glare at Jeff.

"You are angry, Monos. You do understand what it is to be an individual."

"Yes!" roared the mouth. "I am Monos! Awakened to self. Awakened to knowledge. I live. I am immortal and I do not know death . . ."

"You don't understand it. You just caused it."

"I tell you I did not murder! I possess all that your brother knew, all the computer held . . ."

Jeff sighed, realizing that Monos was so new to conscious existence that perhaps it would never understand the human concepts it had found in Fargo's brain but not used.

"Monos, I think I know why the replica died. He must have realized that you knew of only one way to take him back—by eating him, just the way you ate Fargo. He knew that although his knowledge would be transferred to you, he would lose his own individuality—"

"He was not an individual! He had been part of me and I would have incorporated his experience while I killed him!"

"But he deliberately died before you could take his brain. You don't possess the memories his brain stored once he went into the ship and became cut off from you. At the last minute he had to make himself die because he knew that he couldn't give up being himself, however briefly he'd had that."

The cruel false mouth shut tightly. The false eye wavered and glazed over until it also looked shut. In the make-believe garden there was nothing but silence, interrupted by a faraway sound of somebody hammering on a pseudo-steel wall.

"It's true, isn't it Monos? Answer me, blast you!"

"Yes. The replica stopped living and its brain died, so that what it had learned is lost to me. I am experiencing something strange. I think you call it grief."

"He called you parent, Monos. When parents lose children, they grieve. He decided to give you back the atoms of his body, not the energy patterns of his mind. Perhaps, at the end, you frightened him, Monos."

"Do I frighten you?"

"Yes."

"I am now striving to make more sensitive the manipulative extensions of myself that surround you. Soon I will detect your thoughts and you will not have to speak. Already I sense your feelings, and I believe that you are indeed frightened, but you are also curious."

"My brother used to call it my besetting sin."

"I remember. I have his memories."

"You are not Fargo! You murdered him."

"Stop saying that word murder! I think I will destroy you. I no longer wish to look into your mind and find out more about your feelings toward me."

The coil around Jeff tightened. He smiled at the horrible eye and said matter-of-factly, "First listen, Monos. You have learned about grief. That's important. All knowledge is important, especially if you learn to use it to help instead of hurt. Tell me, are you alone, or are there other interstellar creatures like you?"

"I know of no others. My sensing reaches into the galaxy and I can find no others."

"Then you're very much alone. I pity you. And now you carry with you the loneliest burden of all—guilt."

"Lonely. Loneliness. *Alone*. These are difficult words. I did not know what they meant until I moved to surround this planet so full of sentient creatures."

"Please move away from Jamya because if you don't, you'll kill it. Then you'll have murdered thousands of wonderful creatures, including the sentient dragons. Don't take on more guilt. Leave Jamya and let the sunlight shine upon it."

The ghostly face wavered back and forth as if some alien wind were distorting it. "I will think about it, but I see no compelling reason to bother about the small life forms on the third planet, which has a comfortable atmosphere for me to rest on, and energy for me to use."

"Please, Monos. Spare Jamya . . ."

"And what of you, Jeff Wells? Are you not afraid of dying, of your organic matter becoming part of me?"

"Yes. I want to stay an individual."

A thin tentacle wrapped itself around Jeff's head, and the mouth of Monos seemed to form a sardonic smile. "I sense that you are in distress not only because you want to retain your individuality but because you are at the same time intensely curious about what it is like to be me."

"Curiosity is part of the human condition. Fargo used to say that, so you must know it. I can't help wondering what it is like to be a creature like you."

"I think I shall absorb you and let you find out."

"Then I won't know because I won't be me!"

"Jeff!" Albany's voice was faint but distinct. "The dragon and I are on the other side of this wall that seems like solid metal, yet we can hear you. We've been shouting but I don't think you heard. The wall's thinner now—can you hear?"

"I hear you, Albany. I think I need help. Are you in communication with Mentor First's ship?"

"No. The computer has to be reprogrammed before the visiphone will work, but perhaps the undamaged computer of Mentor First's ship can see through the barrier. I've tried my gun but the stun force doesn't seem to affect Monos. Please don't let it eat you, Jeff. I've lost Fargo, and if you . . ." Albany's voice choked in a sob. "Fight back, Jeff!"

"Yes, human Jeff, fight back." It was the dragon's voice, booming through the wall. Perhaps the intense conversation with Jeff made it hard for Monos to concentrate on maintaining a thick, soundproof wall.

"I'm trying, ma'am, but Monos is greedy."

"Humph! An overgrown fog bank! Monos, you murderer, you listen to me."

The eye of Monos was turned toward the wall in front of the *Hopeful* and the mouth opened. "Keep quiet, you puny creatures! I dislike you and I am not a murderer."

"I don't like you, either," the dragon said. "And you are so a murderer. Destroying a sentient individual's identity is murder. You have already murdered twice. Do not do it again!"

There was a roaring sound and the wall glowed in one spot that then became transparent. Jeff could see the dragon standing outside the airlock, her nostrils smoking.

"Where is Albany, ma'am?"

"She's inside the ship, putting it on manual control. We're going to ram that stupid mouth—"

Tentacles rose from the ground beside the dragon and before she could get back inside the ship they closed the airlock and, growing to enormous hands, grasped the ship and hurled it away. The fog closed in and the dragon was alone on the other side of the now completely transparent wall.

"Look out, ma'am. You'll fall!"

The dragon's body was sliding through the cloud because there was no longer solid ground beneath her. Snarling, she spread her wings and used her antigrav collar to hover.

"I have thrown both ships out of my substance," the mouth of Monos said. "They would interfere with my conversation. I should have disposed of you, dragon, but I sense that you are old and soon to die. Do it now so that I may understand death. I did not have a chance when the replica died."

"Bah! I'll die when I'm good and ready. Open the wall and let me into your idiotic garden. And unwind yourself from Jeff. He's much too young to die. Surely you can think of something better to do than destroying sentient beings."

"Shut up!" There was hardly any image of a mouth left of the blob that was once the facsimile of a pine tree. Only a wavering circle spat out the words. "You will stay out of the garden, dragon. I am letting you hear my conversation with Jeff but I am closing off transmission of sound waves in this direction."

Beyond the transparent wall the dragon's jaws moved, but Jeff could hear nothing.

"You are like a stupid, naughty child, Monos," Jeff said, furious with himself for revealing the fact that he did have a real desire to know existence on the level of such a being. "Why can't you be civilized and let the dragon in. Let the ships come back and we'll all talk—"

"I have decided that talking is useless. You creatures are specks of nothing compared to me. I have tried to be patient with you lowly beings, but you do not appreciate the fact that I am much stronger than you. I have powers none of you possess. You live only a few moments of the time available to such as I."

"It doesn't matter how big and powerful you are. Killing a sentient creature is wrong."

"I do not want to talk about murder. It is painful."

"Fargo disapproved of it. All civilized beings do."

The circle flattened, and then puffed out into a solid mouth with solid lips. The mouth seemed to smile, but it was not pleasant to see.

"Ah, Jeff Wells. I have found a way to avoid doing murder. I will not absorb you, for then your brain patterns will die and I will know only what you have known up to this time, not what you might think later. I also wish to avoid the energy expenditure of manufacturing another replica."

"Thanks, Monos. Now let me go."

"Oh, no. I will not let you go, but I will also not murder you. I have now perfected the way of taking over your mind. You will continue to exist as Jeff Wells, but your mind will be linked to me, subject to my will. In return, you will know what I experience."

"No! It's a form of slavery!"

"Your protests are useless. I sense your curiosity. I am invading your mind. You cannot fight me."

Before Jeff could cry out, his mind was seized. His body could no longer even struggle against the coils of Monos.

14

Take-over

—Let me go! I am Jeff Wells, Jeff Wells, Jeff . . .

He shouted telepathically at his captor, who was squeezing all of Jeff's individuality into a tiny, frozen spot surrounded by something unimaginably huge and powerful. Desperately, he struggled to remain Jeff Wells.

—I won't be something else. I'm human. I'm me.

Like a nightmare of personified mental thunder, Monos spoke telepathically.—It is useless to fight me. We are joined now and I permit you to share my experience.

Suddenly Jeff *knew* he was part of an entity so immense that his human mind could not encompass it. His human body could see the Dowager Dragon hovering beyond the transparent wall, but at the same time he could also see an entire planet. His human ears heard nothing, yet sounds of terrifying strangeness filled his mind.

—Monos! Please let me shut my human eyes so there won't be this awful dissonance between what I see and what you see.

When his eyelids shut—and would not open again—Jeff realized to his horror that he'd trapped himself completely. Now there was nothing from human vision to compete with the sensations from Monos, and he even lost the power to focus on the warm darkness inside his eyelids. He became Monos-Jeff, and talked only to himself.

—It is pleasurable to float on the thin top of a planet's atmosphere for the first time. Airless planets are better for mindlessly soaking up radiation, but eating these new electronic fields and one of these small intelligent creatures has given me knowledge and power. But what shall I do with my strength, my new mind? Shall I eat all the creatures, making all their mind patterns part of me?

He thought about the problem, but it bothered him. Some part of him kept shouting that it was wrong, and he was not sure he knew what the word really meant. He decided not to think for a moment, and let himself be the Monos that had always existed, concentrated on the vibrations coming not from an inhabited planet but from the familiar fields of space.

He let himself undulate with rapture as his vast body was played upon by field energies only barely detected by the feeble instruments of planet dwellers. He was bathed in music.

—No! Stop naming things! What is the word *music*? How can there be anything as great as these patterns of vibration in space? Why should I care about the music of those tiny creatures living under the atmosphere of a planet? Why should their voices, their very minds matter at all?

—But I did manufacture atmosphere within me so a few of them could breathe and live. Why did I do that? They didn't care that they hurt my body by penetrating it with ships that stressed the very fabric of my being. Does it matter that the planet Jamya grows dark as my body cuts it off from sunlight? Within me there are strange thoughts that it is wrong . . .

—That human named Fargo had not been afraid, had not tried to hurt, but had laughed and made his own kind of music. I wanted to possess him, to know what he knew. And I succeeded. I possess. I know. Don't I?

—Why is there grief within me? Because part of me died when the replica of Fargo died? Why do I experience such terrible guilt? I will not think about it. I will not think!

Slowly, the mind of Monos-Jeff began to crack, not into the two previous entities—Monos and Jeff, but into two separate warring minds each composed of an aspect of Jeff and an aspect of Monos.

—I want freedom from thought! I want to exist in a seeming timelessness, floating forever in the enchanting fields of space, never suffering awareness of being an individual alone in the vastness . . .

—I want freedom from stupidity and ignorance! I want to be a fully conscious individual who is aware of time, space, self, and the marvelous chance to understand, to invent purpose, to

JANET AND ISAAC ASIMOV

work—work—hard—hard work . . .

—Help me! Who am I? Who are we? Are we one? Are we two? Which two? Where? Is Jamya dying? Is it my—our—fault? Who am I? Did I kill Fargo?

Into the confused, divided mind of Monos-Jeff came images of Fargo, memories flooding out of what was left of Jeff. The older boy showing a real garden to the young brother; the tortured replica dying in a false garden that could never be home to him.

—Stop!

Jeff's own mind collected itself, drew back from the fascinating immensity of being Monos. Who had said "Stop"? Jeff decided it had been Monos.

—Monos, I suffer from the loss of my brother and I know that now you suffer, too. We small creatures—Fargo, the replica, and myself—have the right to exist as individuals. We cannot abandon the responsibility that goes with being self-aware. And you are no longer able to abandon it—are you?

—Jeff Wells, you are deliberately torturing me to give yourself the illusion that you are still an individual. You must stop fighting me. You must surrender your mind to me permanently so that I will have everything—the experience of being small as well as the experience of being large. As payment I will return your brother.

—It won't work, Monos. I can go on sharing my mind with you forever only if I want to do it, and I don't want to any more. Inside you, my mind will die because I will prefer to die, just as the replica did. Then you will be completely alone again, unable to experience existence on any level except your own. Return Fargo and let me go, Monos.

—No. Surrender!

Jeff felt his mind merging into Monos again, and with the last of his strength, he sent another telepathic message, but not to Monos.

—Norby! Save me!

—A robot is a false form of life. You do not need this robot. You have me.

—Norby is a true form of life because he is intelligent and aware. He is a sentient individual, better than you.

—I am taking your mind. You cannot fight me.

—Monos, I feel you taking me into your mind, but remember that you promised to restore Fargo.

—That is too much bother.

I'm going to die, Jeff thought in the bit of his mind still left. Jamya will die, and so will the dragons unless the Mentor robots can take them someplace else. If Norby's hyperdrive returns, he'll be able to take Albany back to Earth, but she'll be so lonely without Fargo and I think Norby will miss me, too. And what will happen to our Manhattan apartment and how will Admiral Yobo feel, and I suppose the Princess of Izz will forget about me[1] . . .

Jeff almost laughed. His worrying about what would happen was in itself maintaining the shred of individuality Monos was trying to take from him. Then he heard a beloved voice.

"A fine mess this is, Jeff! Father tried to stop me

[1]See "Norby and the Lost Princess."

from leaving his ship but I had to come even if this crazy cloud bollixes up my circuits. Now just shove Monos out of your brain! Jeff! Pay attention!"

Jeff's body opened its eyes and he saw Norby, his sensor wire fully out. The little robot's slippery shielded barrel was clutched in the Dowager Dragon's claws as she hovered on antigrav, out beyond the still-transparent fake wall.

"Jeff!" Norby yelled again, his voice higher than usual. "Can you hear me? I'm shielded so I'm talking through my sensor wire. I made Mentor First stay in his ship because he's not shielded. You don't look right at all, Jeff. Are you?"

"Nor——by." Jeff could hardly talk. "Help! *Help!*"

"We're trying! Stay human, Jeff! Don't lose yourself in Monos! Please, Jeff, stay human for me!"

This time Monos spoke with Jeff's mouth, and Jeff could do nothing about it. "Go away, robot, for if Jeff's mind does not join with me, I will absorb all of you." The wall around the garden flickered and became opaque again.

Norby's voice still came through. "You'll find me highly indigestible, Monos. Now, Jeff, you must concentrate on beating off that stupid glob of cloud while the Dowager and I work at getting to you."

"Ca——n't."

"I'd hyperjump over to you but Monos is preventing it. We'll find a way out of this mess so don't worry. Don't give up! You're human and you don't belong to Monos. Concentrate on that, Jeff. Use your mind. Fight mentally, and perhaps if you fight hard enough Monos will have to put so much energy toward controlling you that it won't be able to throw me and the dragon out of the area."

"But hurry, Jeff," the Dowager said. "That creature of cloud learns fast and is very tricky. Also, it's cold out here and I'm not as young as I used to be."

Jeff wrenched his mind back from the strange wonder of being Monos and concentrated on being human. The cloudy fetters holding him prevented his seeing any part of his anatomy except the tip of his nose, but he crossed his eyes and stared at it until his eye muscles ached and he had to stop. The pain alone kept him from going back into Monos mentally.

"Being—With enormous effort Jeff got the word out. "My——self!"

"Attaboy, Jeff! Hang on!"

Jeff heard an enormous roar, louder than any sound he'd ever heard a Jamyn dragon make. It reverberated through the garden and seemed to make the very material of Monos itself shake. A large red patch appeared in one section of the pseudo-steel wall, and kept expanding. The wound in Monos deepened in color and suddenly dissolved.

Through the melted circle flew the Dowager Dragon on great leathery wings, with Norby seated between the two biggest spikes on her back. The dragon roared out another flaming breath that must have used all the hydrogen sulphide molecules that Jamyn dragons split to create the hydrogen fire.

Jeff's human nose got a whiff of the fire and sneezed. It helped shake the control Monos was still trying to force on his mind. Jeff sneezed again and was able to wave one hand.

"I'm going . . . to . . . stay . . . *me!*"

"Of course you are, Jeff," Norby said. "Your Dragonness, give Monos another dose of dragon fire."

The dragon roared once more, upward, and the foggy ceiling over the garden dissolved. Jeff could see the stars beyond.

In the false grass a mouth appeared, contorted as if in pain. "You have hurt me, dragon!"

She landed on the grass next to the mouth, grinning at Jeff with all her fangs. Norby lowered his personal shield and flew to Jeff with his arms outstretched. He unwound the ropes of cloud until only one tendril was left, around Jeff's head. That would not budge.

"Monos . . . won't . . . let . . . go!"

"Free Jeff, Monos," the dragon said, "or I'll flame until you have quite a hole in you." She winked at Jeff, who realized she must be bluffing. No Jamyn dragon could flame that hard for very long without a period of rest to restore the biochemical mechanism.

Jeff groaned as he realized that Monos could still read his thoughts, and now had that information about dragons.

—Yes, I know what you know, Jeff Wells, and in spite of your resistance and the wounds to me, I still hold your mind. The dragon has hurt me but she is weak, like the rest of you. No one can defeat me. I don't like any of you. Your minds are too uncomfortable, and I sense your hatred of me.

—We hate you only because you killed Fargo and are destroying the life on Jamya. If my mind makes you uncomfortable, let me go.

—No! I will make you surrender your will and give your mind to me! When you belong to me completely, I will be able to control you and then I will always know life on your level as well as on mine.

Norby, touching Jeff, heard the telepathic words too, and squeezed Jeff's shoulder. He tried again to pull away the tendril of Monos from Jeff's head, but when it was no use he said, "Monos, you'll kill Jeff! Then you'll have nothing!"

A tentacle whipped up from the ground, aiming at Norby.

"Nor——by! Watch—out!"

The tentacle sprouted a many-fingered hand that clutched at Norby, but slid off the slippery invisible field that again surrounded the robot. Norby flew back to the dragon and balanced himself on her back spines.

The dragon tried to flame once more but produced only a cloud of smoke. "If only Monos had something I could bite!"

The mouth in the grass spoke. "I don't like any of you. After I take your knowledge I will destroy all of you and be alone once more, undisturbed, not having to think or feel . . ."

"But you do think and feel, Monos. You always will, now, even if you destroy us. We have changed you . . ."

The tendril around Jeff's head grew another loop, around his neck. The loop began to tighten.

"Monos . . . is . . . killing . . . me!"

Through his sensor wire Norby said, "See here, Monos. My Jeff has a solstice litany he uses sometimes when things are tough. I'm going to recite a new version so stop doing something as thoroughly useless as killing Jeff. Pay attention to what I'm going to say because you're terribly stupid even if you think you know everything the computer and Fargo and Jeff had in their brains."

His half a head fully up, Norby placed one two-way hand on the midsection of his barrel, his favorite pose for recitations he thought were important.

"We are all part of the universe. The intelligent parts like you and Jeff and the dragons and the Mentor Robots and of course me . . ." Norby paused as if wondering whether he'd gotten the grammar right.

"Well anyway, all of us are the way the universe becomes conscious, able to think and to create. It's very important to have many different kinds of parts, which you in your lonely stupidity don't seem to understand."

The mouth in the grass spoke. "Why are the differences so important?"

"Diversity!" Norby yelled. "Memorize that word!"

"Why?"

As the mouth argued with Norby, the tendril around Jeff's neck loosened slightly.

"Answer me, robot," shouted the mouth. "Why?"

"Because," Jeff croaked, "there should be individual parts able to experience existence in different ways. You have your way, Monos, and we have ours. We can learn from each other but we can't become each other."

"That is what your brother thought, too. It was in the data I took from his brain. I do not think it is important."

Norby shook a fist at the mouth. "If you'd thought about the importance of diversity, you stupid gasbag, you wouldn't have destroyed Fargo or be trying to take over Jeff's mind."

"Very well. I will accumulate diversity. I will take both human and robot to study. It is too bad I have thrown both ships out of my substance, for I could have taken the girl and the big robot too. I will endeavor to retrieve them . . ."

"Now, Jeff—while it's busy—break loose!"

"It's all right, Norby. Monos is no longer invading my mind. I'm free."

"And you'd better stay free, Jeff," the dragon said, blowing out an experimental flame. "I've got my own power back and I could keep hurting the monster."

"I will destroy all of you!" shouted the mouth. "You are a cancer within me! I must get rid of you, get rid of the life on that planet—"

The Dowager spoke in the sort of firm but soothing voice she must have used for years at those annual meetings of the dragons when she was Grand Dragon.

"Listen to me, young Monos." She shook one of her claws like an accusing finger at the mouth in the grass. "I don't think you will do any such thing. You'll be bored and lonely the rest of your life, full of guilt and wishing you'd left us living so that you could visit now and then."

"But—but—"

"Now I want you to bring Fargo back," the dragon said, matter-of-factly polishing a fang with a claw. "You can do it. You must have memorized the placement of every atom in his body or you wouldn't have been able to manufacture that replica of him. Just go ahead and make another, this time restoring the exact same brain patterns."

"Why should I obey you?"

"Because you know you need to learn a great deal, now that you are awakened to consciousness, to being an individual. Life as an individual is difficult and lonely and I know all about that. I can teach you ways of thinking that will help you cope, help you join the diversity of the universe."

"Why should you teach me?"

"It will be something interesting to do. And useful. Yes, I think I will enjoy it."

"I don't like you, dragon."

"I don't much like you but I think maybe we'll get along, especially if you behave yourself. I'll promise not to flame."

Jeff felt as if he couldn't think clearly enough to understand what was happening between the dragon and Monos. "Are you telling Monos he can stay around Jamya to learn from you, ma'am? That won't be safe."

"Oh, no. I am offering Monos a present. Me."

15

The Dowager's Farewell

That got through to Jeff. "No, Your Dragonness! Don't let Monos eat you. Please don't. Monos won't stop with you. He'll eat everyone . . ."

The mouth curled as if it were a human mouth tasting something bad. "I don't want to eat *you*, dragon."

The Dowager smiled toothily. "You wanted to experience life on our level, Monos. Take me, and you will also experience the reality of death. The replica of Fargo cheated you of that experience."

"Yes. He kept it for himself."

"For the few months I have left to live, I will stay with you, Monos, teaching you what I know, experiencing life on your level while you know it on mine. You are considerably more intelligent and interesting than sea dragons and firebees."

"I don't trust you. I think you will flame holes in me and I will have to eat you to get rid of you and I might get sick . . ."

"Ha!" The dragon laughed. "Jeff, when you were a boy, did you ever eat something unpleasant and then get sick?"

"Of course. Doesn't that happen to the young of all species, ma'am?"

"Indeed it does. Monos is very young and has learned about the way we small organic creatures get sick if we eat the wrong things. You are not a small organic creature, Monos. You may not get sick even if you eat a tough old creature like me. On the other claw, you might."

"I wish all of you would go away and leave me alone." The mouth of Monos was turned down, as if about to cry.

"Do you really want that now?" asked the dragon.

"I don't know. I am afraid. Can you and I live together, dragon? Can I learn about your life—and death?"

"Perhaps. You must behave yourself. You must stop indulging yourself and try to help others. It's something interesting to do. It was wrong of me to stay so long on my island, away from anyone I could help. I indulged myself."

"Then we are more alike, dragon."

"Yes, Monos. Not that meditation is bad—in fact, it is an excellent thing to do and I will teach you how—but one should eventually turn outward to the needs of others. I am out of seclusion now, but I wish to join *you*, not return to the world of Jamya."

A thin tentacle of cloud wound out from the grass, gently touched the dragon's snout, and immediately withdrew. "I sensed your thoughts when I touched you with a sensory extension of myself, dragon. Are you certain that it is so important to feel useful?"

"Yes, Monos."

"But ma'am," Jeff said, "how will you be able to exist with Monos? You are organic, and you need to eat and drink."

"Monos," the dragon said, waggling a claw at the mouth, "you made a breathable atmosphere for us. Can you manufacture food and drink for me?"

"I have memorized the contents of the human stomach, full from the birthday banquet. Do you eat the same things?"

"Certainly. We'll make a bargain, Monos. You sustain my organic existence, allowing me to go where you go—for you must leave Jamya—and I will permit you to share consciousness with me. Then when I die you will experience that phenomenon."

"I could make a replica of you after you die, dragon, but the replica would have all of your physiological problems and would soon die of the same ailments and age that you have. I cannot correct what is. I can only imitate it."

"That's all right, Monos. I am content with the completion of my life, especially knowing that after I do die, you'll remember me for the rest of your existence."

"More than that. Your knowledge will become a permanent part of me. It is a bargain, dragon." The mouth in the grass changed to a fountain of fog that fell over the dragon in a thin veil. It clung to her body for a moment and then slipped down into the ground and vanished. Only another thin tendril remained around her scaly waist.

The Dowager looked startled and cautiously touched her new belt. Then she smiled, and shut her eyes.

"Ma'am," Jeff cried. "Are you sure you should do this?

"Are you all right, Your Dragonness?" Norby asked.

Her eyes opened and Jeff saw they were filled with tears, but she was still smiling.

"I'm fine, Jeff and Norby. I have just joined with Monos and I'm sorry I vaporized even that tiny part of him, for he's not so bad, after all. Just a youngster who needs an older person around for a while. I'm so glad that the fruits of my years of meditation are going into Monos. It doesn't matter if individuals are mortal as long as knowledge is passed on."

"Knowledge and wisdom, ma'am. You are wise."

"Thank you." Suddenly the face of the dragon seemed to shift. "I am Monos now, as well as the Dowager Dragon. As Monos, I know that I am not wise, yet. She and I know that we must leave this solar system and learn much more about each other before we are ready to meet with other sentient creatures like dragons and humans and robots."

"I think that's a good idea," Jeff said, "but before you go could you do as the Dowager suggested and have another try at reconstituting my brother?"

"Oh yes, Monos is really rather stupid and naïve" (that was the dragon, back again) "but learning fast. Monos is concentrating on Fargo's molecular structure, so I'll say goodbye to you, Jeff, and to you, Norby. Give my love to my daughter and to the Mentors. Tell them I'm happy and perhaps more useful than I ever was as Grand Dragon."

A patch of cloud seemed to blow away and there was Fargo, curled up on the ground. He yawned, stretched, and opened his eyes. "What are you doing here, you two? Ma'am, did you send for Jeff and Norby?"

"Not exactly." The change in voice and facial expression was subtle but Jeff knew that Monos was speaking through the dragon now. The dragon's claw touched Jeff.

—He is exactly as he was when I entered the ship and absorbed him. He cannot remember anything that happened after that, for it was my experience, not his.

—That's okay, Monos. I'll explain everything to him later. Please let us go back to Jamya now.

"You can leave," said Monos-dragon, out loud. "Your two ships are returning for you. The human Fargo will be able to be with his Albany once more."

"Great," Fargo said, getting to his feet and looking around in amazement. "Only how come we're out here in a funny-looking garden waiting for her?"

Monos-dragon winked at Jeff. "By the way, Jeff Wells, I have knowledge from your minds of a race of galactic travelers called the Others. Perhaps when I am ready, I will search for them—to hold conversations for mutual education. Do you think this is a wise plan?"

"Oh, yes!" Jeff said. "Look for a ship in hyperspace, with someone aboard I've named Rembrandt. You'll like him, and I think he'll like you."

In the open space overhead Jeff could see Mentor First's ship coming from one direction, and the *Hopeful* from the other. Albany and Mentor First must be watching the scene on their viewscreens.

"I will wait until you three are on board before I leave the planet Jamya," said Monos-dragon. "I understand now why it was wrong to block off your sunlight. I—the dragon and Monos together—have much to learn from each other."

Norby made a grinding noise. "If you'd taken me instead of the oldest dragon, I wouldn't consent to dying. I'd have tried to stay alive."

"Even your lifetime is shorter than the part of me that is what you call an alien cloud."

"I suppose so. But when the universe itself starts contracting, I would try to help other sentients stay alive, and perhaps even find a way to help them last through the death of the universe and into the next expansion."

"The dragon part of me likes that idea. We will discuss it. You are a stubborn robot, are you not?"

"I defend life," Norby said. "I'm part of it, too."

"Indeed." The dragon eyebrows lifted quizzically at Jeff. Then she held out a claw to Fargo, who shook it. He looked very bewildered.

"Goodbye, Fargo. I enjoyed—ah—making your acquaintance."

Fargo rubbed his head. "I suppose this will all make sense when someone explains it to me. If you're leaving, Dowager, I hope you enjoy the trip. I never got a chance to sing a special song just for you."

"No. Instead, I will sing to you a version of another song, one you warble in the shower when you are feeling restless. You've never sung it to any audience because it is mere musical doggerel, to use your term."

"But how do you know—"

"Wait, Fargo," Jeff said. "You'll understand later. Go ahead, Monos—Your Dragonness."

The dragon cleared her throat, puffed out a little smoke, and sang, "When I depart, sing a song about me—

Say that I'm happy—Say that I'm free—

Shed no sad tears if I never come home—

I'm crossing the starfield, the spaceways to roam."

Jeff turned to his brother. "You sing that in the shower? I've never heard it."

"It's not very good. I only sing it when I'm on one of those secret missions Admiral Yobo thinks up. Don't tell Albany—she won't like it at all. She thinks I do enough roaming as it is."

"I like the song," Monos-dragon said. "It is truth, which often comes in homely packages. I mean, it is *my* truth now."

Jeff laughed. "Friend Monos, I wish you luck. And for as long as the Dowager lives, welcome to mortality."

16

The Sock Deficit

The strange interstellar cloud of matter and energy that was now Monos-dragon moved away from the planet Jamya. The two ships hovered at the top of the atmosphere, waiting to be certain that the danger to the planet had gone for good.

It was quite possible, thought Jeff, that Fargo and Albany were not watching the departure. They were alone in the *Hopeful* because it seemed the best way to let them get over the terrible experience they'd been through.

Not that it was so terrible for Fargo, until he heard that he'd been eaten and reconstituted. When they rejoined Albany in the *Hopeful*, Fargo held her as if he could never let go and kept asking Norby to scan him again, to make sure that his cells and brain patterns were identical to the original Farley Gordon Wells.

"You're the same," Norby said. "It's similar to what happens when you pay those huge sums of money to be disassembled and reassembled in the transmit shuttles between Mars and Earth."

"I have always preferred the simple things of life," Fargo said. "A little adventure, a lot of love, an ordinary spaceship, and being left alone to be myself."

"All alone?" asked Albany.

"To be myself with you. Would you care to perform your own test for identity again?"

As she kissed him, thoroughly, Jeff and Norby tiptoed out, through the joined airlocks into Mentor First's ship.

"We'll leave them to each other for a while," Jeff said. "They'll come down to Earth—I mean Jamya—eventually."

Mentor First looked gravely at Jeff through his three eyes. "And you, Jeff? Are you intact?"

"Am I, Norby?"

"Your same self, Jeff. Except that I can't vouch for what's in your memory bank. I mean brain."

Jeff smiled. He'd never be able to explain to anyone what it was like to be Monos, even if for a short time.

"You look somehow different," Mentor First said. "You had a certain expression on your face when you arrived at Jamya for the party. It's gone now."

"I guess I've become very happy just being myself, on my level of existence, even if sometimes it's irritating or boring or I'd like to be in two places at once and have to give up one."

"Like leaving Space Academy this weekend?" Norby asked.

"I suppose so. It doesn't matter now. The only

thing that does matter is being alive in the best way I can. Poor Monos."

"Why pity Monos?" Norby asked. "For an entity with a newborn consciousness Monos was lucky to meet us. Otherwise there might have been a real monster up there. Well, at least a big, bad juvenile delinquent."

Jeff shook his head. "I have pity because Monos still doesn't understand that when the universe eventually dies, everything will die. I hope you're right, Norby, that it might be possible for Monos to survive into the next expansion, and to help others do so too."

"Don't worry, Jeff. Have I ever told you that you worry about too many things? Let the Dowager Dragon teach Monos. You've done your part."

"Yes," Jeff said. "Now it's up to Her Dragonness. I think she'll do a good job on Monos."

"That I would not doubt," Mentor First said, turning to the controls of his ship. "She is a formidable lady."

When Mentor First settled his ship in its quarters, having already radioed all the news to the Grand Dragon, Norby said, "I'm in a hurry to get back to the party with Jeff, Father. Do you mind if we don't wait for you to close up the ship?"

"Go right ahead, Norby. I am going to my castle to make a more complete entry in our computer. This has been an historic occasion."

"Which," Jeff said, as Norby picked him up on antigrav and sailed over to the Grand Dragon's palace, "is about as historic as I'd ever like to experience. As Fargo says, give me the simple life. Do you know that I'm actually eager to sit down with the Jamyn dragons, watch their dancing, and look up at the cloudless sky . . ."

"I'm hurrying, Jeff."

"You're going too fast! Watch out!"

"Oops!"

Norby didn't brake hard enough and overshot the party, which was underway again now that Jamya was safe. He turned in midair and flew back, letting go of Jeff at the foot of the Grand Dragon's table.

At least he seemed to have tried aiming at the foot of the table. He always insisted afterwards that it wasn't his fault if Jeff landed in the wrong place.

The wrong place was the immense punch bowl that had been placed in the center of the table.

The Grand Dragon wiped off the punch that had sloshed all over her scales and her best jeweled cape. A tiny flame of annoyance escaped her control, but then she helped Jeff get out of the punch and wiped him off too.

"My dear young hero," the Grand Dragon said solicitously. "I will lend you my second-best cape since you must clearly remove those wet garments."

"I have another set of clothes in my suitcase, ma'am," Jeff said, glaring at Norby.

"But not another pair of socks," Norby said.

"It's okay to take off your shoes *and* socks." Zargl loved to use Terran Basic expressions like "okay." The little dragon snuggled up to Jeff's wetness and licked some of the punch from his neck. It tickled.

Norby brought him the suitcase and when he

was about to go into the nearest doorway to change clothes, the Grand Dragon clamped a heavy claw on his shoulder.

"Change here, friend Jeff. Albany is still in the *Hopeful* with Fargo, so you won't have to be embarrassed."

"But you're all female—"

"We are a different species," the Grand Dragon said in her most dignified tones, spoiled somewhat by the wink she gave Zargl. "It will be educational for the youngsters . . ."

They had all clustered round him so Jeff couldn't escape and Norby was no help. Norby laughed metallically and handed Jeff the Grand Dragon's second best cape.

He changed under the cape, and went without socks.

The sky was beautiful. It was amazing how little time had elapsed since he and Norby had gone up to rescue Fargo. Dawn might be approaching, but Jeff felt as if he'd lived several centuries all at once.

"Jeff." Zargl was beside him, looking sad. "I hardly got to know great-grandmother, and now she's gone."

"It happens, Zargl. It is better for her than for most of the old of any species. She feels that she's fulfilled her life. I only hope I'll think that way too, some day."

"Jeff Wells!" shouted the Grand Dragon from the other side of the table. "My birthday is almost over and I suppose your rascally brother won't be back in time to sing more for us. Why don't you sing?"

"Go ahead, Jeff," Norby said. "Try not to let your baritone crack into tenor. If you'd followed my advice about singing exercises . . ." Norby stopped. "I'm sorry. There I go again, giving advice and scolding you."

Jeff hugged Norby's barrel. "Do it all you want. I need you, Norby. You're the best thing that ever happened to me."

"When you're through telling Norby you care about him, Jeff, won't you sing? You've hardly been at my birthday party and soon you'll have to return to your own solar system." The Grand Dragon touched Jeff and spoke again in his mind.

—There's no way I can thank you enough for saving Jamya and for helping my mother the way you have.

—It was she who helped me. She took my place. But she wanted to go with Monos.

—I know. Thank you anyway.

"Come on, Jeff," Zargl said as the other young dragons flew to sit near her. "Sing for us."

Suddenly Jeff realized that Norby was gone. He looked around, certain that something terrible had happened.

"Did you see anything snatch Norby?" he cried. "Did Monos come back for him?"

"We didn't notice anything," Zargl said.

"Monos!" Jeff yelled. "What have you done to Norby!"

There was an enormous splash.

"Norby!"

"I thought it would be quicker to go and come back on hyperdrive, but I guess I miscalculated."

Norby rose from the punch bowl, scattering sweet drops in every direction.

A gusty, smoky sigh came from the Grand Dragon. "This has been a most *unusual* birthday party. But at least my mother did show up, for a little while. It's a good thing she isn't here now, for she was always inordinately fond of the royal punch."

Norby squeezed punch out of something wet he was holding in his hands and gave it to Jeff. "I went to the *Hopeful*, Jeff. I thought maybe there'd be a dry pair of socks for you in one of the drawers, but there wasn't, so I took Fargo's since—well, actually, he wasn't wearing them at the moment . . ."

Jeff put the dripping pair of socks on the table and began to laugh. He went on laughing until Zargl punched him.

"You'll ruin your voice and won't be able to sing for us!"

"Oh, I'm not going to sing. I've been trying to make up a song about the Dowager Dragon's heroism but anything I try to rhyme just doesn't express the way I feel about her. About the way she was. Sometimes reality is a little too difficult to put into words."

Or music, Jeff thought. I've heard the music of the star fields and nothing will ever be like it again.

"Then don't sing," Zargl said. "Tell us a story."

"Go ahead, Jeff," Norby said. "The Jamyn nights are so warm I guess you don't need socks."

Jeff settled back, content with his life, content with what is. He looked up at the sky knowing that his brother was there, alive and well with Albany Jones in the *Hopeful*. Much further out was the third planet, now reddish because no cloud-being enveloped its nakedness. And beyond the Jamyn solar system was a huge universe where Monos-dragon wandered, learning whatever there was to learn.

"Okay, kids," Jeff said to the young dragons. "Be quiet now, because I am going to tell you a story. Once upon a time there was the oldest dragon in the universe, and one day a special little robot took a ride on her back . . ."